T0027219

A Dragon's Passion

Sandra Enriquez

iUniverse, Inc.
Bloomington

A Dragon's Passion

Copyright © 2012 Sandra Enriquez

This is a work of fiction. All of the characters, names, incidents, organizations, and dialogue in this novel are either the products of the author's imagination or are used fictitiously.

iUniverse books may be ordered through booksellers or by contacting:

iUniverse
1663 Liberty Drive
Bloomington, IN 47403
www.iuniverse.com
1-800-Authors (1-800-288-4677)

ISBN: 978-1-4759-2559-3 (sc)
ISBN: 978-1-4759-2560-9 (hc)
ISBN: 978-1-4759-2561-6 (e)

Library of Congress Control Number: 2012908354

Printed in the United States of America

iUniverse rev. date: 8/14/2012

Dedication

To my children, Mianna and Evan; this was written to help you understand that not everything in life is easy, but you will always have the unconditional love you need to help you along the way.

To my husband, Joseph, my mom, Yvonne, and friends; Jo-Deane and Krista, your encouragement has meant more to me than you will ever know!

Prologue

Land of Miradel, Petroset Kingdom
New Kingdom Year 427

"I will teach King Claude that justice denied will cost him more than he expects!"

My mother was really angry. I had never seen her so mad, and she was scaring me. I understood what the teacher did to me was bad, but she was turning red and shaking all over now. She had not even done that when I told her what happened in the classroom.

"Tyson, go to your bed! I have something I need to take care of, and I do not want to have to worry any more about your safety."

I knew better than to argue when my mother was like this. I got up out of the corner I was hiding in and ran to my straw bed that was in a small, carved out corner beside the fireplace and let the fabric sheet down to keep me safe from any more angry looks.

I heard the door slam shut and I closed my eyes. The tears came, and I could not stop them. *Was I ever going to stop having nightmares?*

The one thing I remember from the day in the king's court was the round, blue eyes of the King's daughter, who was just shy of reaching her first year, from what I could tell, based on the other children I knew from my village that looked similar. She smiled at me the whole time. Her eyes never looked away, and that made me feel special for those few minutes. *Was she always in the king's court?* The King seemed upset that she was there. He yelled at the lady to take her out of the room. I do not think he likes his daughter. I think the King's daughter and I have something in common; a father who does not love you.

First Kiss

1

Land of Miradel, Petroset Kingdom
New Kingdom Year 445

"Father, I do not care that I am nineteen and well beyond the age considered traditional for marriage. That ship sailed more than several years ago. Nor do I care about the curse that has bound me to the other five princes of Miradel. I will only marry a man that I love and who loves me in return. That is the very least I should be entitled to, given it is your fault the curse even exists!"

My father, King Claude, rose from his seat and strode toward me with an angry scowl on his face. I knew what was going to happen before the blow even hit me on my cheek. I was pretty sure it was going to bruise this time, but I just did not care anymore.

"Annaliessa, you will spend time with the five princes, and you will choose one of them as your husband before your next birthday! Given that we royals are only allowed to be with child once, you must produce an heir. For the other four princes you do not choose, let us hope you have a girl, or they will have to leave Miradel and travel to far off lands to find another princess to marry, or be forced to marry a cousin."

"That wicked witch somehow managed to make a disproportionate number of males be born, limiting our ability to maintain our Kingdom's lineage and security," my father huffed.

"I am not sure why you are complaining, father, it has benefited you greatly these past eighteen years. You hold their very hope of existence in your hands through me. Your scourge of having a daughter rather than a son has, in the end, made you very wealthy and powerful indeed. So, do not forget that I am the one controlling the future of this kingdom the next time you want to strike me. I could easily disappear, and then what will you have?" With that I turned and stomped out of the room. As soon as the door was closed behind me, I ran.

I found myself in the forest on the mountain slopes behind our castle which is in the eastern kingdom of Miradel. The mountain separates us from other lands to the east.

The land of Miradel is a temperate rain forest, rich in resources that other kingdoms long to have access to. However, most were afraid to invade as they did not want to risk being subject to the curse. This also made them reluctant to form covenants with us and allow us to intermarry with them.

¥

I never asked for any of this. You would think I would be happy about five very handsome young men being physically and emotionally attached to me. The fact that they cannot even choose another mate until I have made my selection is only another festering sore to my heart. I have grown up with these men and have been friends with them my whole life, how can anyone expect me to choose one over the other. *If they were not bound to me, would they even like me?* With so many thoughts going through my head, I did not hear him come up behind me.

"What has you so troubled, Annaliessa?" Prince Jordan asked. I jumped at the sound of his voice, and he started to laugh. Jordan was the prince of the southwest kingdom, Vulterrian, which bordered the enormously wide river to the south and the ocean to the west. He was eighteen years, six feet tall, and had light blond hair which he kept short, rather than shoulder length (which was more common), welcoming hazel eyes, and a strong chin and cheekbones. Of course, one of his more alluring features was his well-muscled body. He was rock hard with muscle, and he had the confidence to carry it all, yet without seeming conceited. Out of all the princes, he was by far, my favorite, as he was so easy to talk to. I had always felt comfortable and safe around him. Not that the other princes were unfriendly or reckless, it was just something I could not explain.

"My father is on a rampage again about me getting married."

"Is that why you have a bruise forming on your cheek? I swear, Annaliessa, if he was not your father, and one of the kings, I would have him arrested and beaten for striking you."

"Jordan, believe me, if he was not my father, I would have him arrested and beat him myself."

This garnered a hearty laugh from Jordan. "Remind me to never get on your bad side."

Now it was my turn to laugh. He was good at taking a tense situation and making me smile in spite of it. He was indeed going to make some woman very happy one day. Then the thought that his happiness was dependent on me wiped the smile from my face.

He saw the look of depression and hopelessness descend, and he positioned himself directly in front of me. He took my chin in his hand and brought my head up to look into his eyes. "What is troubling you now, my princess?"

My eyebrow raised in curiosity, "Since when am I *your princess*?"

"You have always been mine; the others just do not know it yet."

"You really are quite full of yourself." I could tell he was playing with me, and was really enjoying himself, too.

He took another step, closing the small gap that had been between us, and wrapped his other arm around my waist, and taking his hand that had been holding my chin and sliding it behind my neck, tangled his fingers in my long blond hair. His mouth closed in on mine and I felt a tingling sensation start from my lips and run down my body. I was receiving my first kiss, and I was not prepared to feel the things he was doing to my body with that kiss. His tongue brushed against my lips and I opened to him, surprising myself with the desire to surrender to his advances. I had not expected to want more of him, and I had to fight back the heat that was coursing through my body, so that I could finally break his hold on me.

"What was that for?" I gasped. "What made you think that it was alright for you to take advantage of me that way?"

"It hardly seemed like I was taking advantage of you. It felt like you enjoyed it as much as I did."

Just then, the other four princes came up on horseback. "There you two are," said Prince Charles, with a look of disapproval on his face. "We have been looking for you."

"We have all been sent by our kingdoms to yours so we can spend some more quality time with the princess," snickered Prince Josiah.

"It looks like Jordan has tried to ingratiate himself to the princess to get a head start on the rest of us," declared Prince Kalvin.

"Prince Samuel, do you not have a snide retort for me as well?" I inquired.

"I think Jordan understands why we would be a bit edgy with him here alone with you."

"Really! Is he someone who is likely to take advantage of a young woman's innocence? You better tell me now, so that I can take extra care when I am without a chaperone in the future."

"Why are you without a chaperone anyway?" asked Charles.

"I had another heart-to-heart talk with my father, and found myself needing to work off a little anger."

"Is the mark you bear on your cheek from your father?" asked Kalvin.

"I guess I should have stopped to grab a cold cloth before making a run for it. Is it really bruising that badly?"

"I have seen worse, but bruises do not belong on the beautiful face of a princess," said Josiah.

"How long are you all here for this time," I questioned?

"A fortnight," stated Jordan simply.

"Well, I guess we better all head back to the castle and start socializing before I end up with a matching bruise on the other cheek."

"Ride with me back to the castle?" asked Jordan.

"I think you and I have had enough one-on-one time today. Samuel, will you allow me to ride back with you?"

Samuel blushed, rendering his normally well-chiseled features to stand out even more. You would think it would take more than a ride with a princess to cause this hulking, six foot one inch man who had just entered his eighteenth year a quarter of a moon cycle ago, to blush, but it made him so endearing. He had close-cropped, brown hair which I think would feel bristly if you were to run your hand over it. I am not certain, of course, as that would be far too forward a thing for me to do, and I had already exceeded my limit in that department today. His golden brown eyes always seemed to have a sparkle to them, making me wonder what he was really thinking.

"Of course, it would be my honor."

Confession

2

Seven days had passed since the princes had left to return to their own kingdoms. It was early in the tree blossom phase of our year, and the time appointed for romance was upon us. I was still trying to figure out how I would choose one of these men to marry. I had made lists of the pluses and minuses for each. I weighed their kingdoms and what they offered to someone like me. I certainly knew who my father favored. He was constantly hinting that Josiah would be a good match for me. In reality, he just wanted control of the river that Josiah's kingdom, Dilentis, being to the southeast provided. They were our closest neighbors, and Josiah's parents were the most pliable to manipulate. My father had sixteen years to get them to bend to his will, and they were starting to get desperate. Josiah did not have any girl cousins to marry, so he was the neediest as far as a marriage to me was concerned: a thought that made my heart ache for him. Josiah was the least "manly" of the five princes, but not in a bad way. He had a slender build, with a longer, thinner face than the other four. He and Kalvin were the shortest of the princes at five foot ten inches. Josiah had spiky brown hair and plain brown eyes. Although he was slender, he carried himself with the confidence of someone twice his size and age, even though he was the youngest of the princes at sixteen. He was an expert negotiator; I guess he made up with words, what he lacked in physical size. I am more inclined to think that he welds more power because of this than any of the other princes. It certainly intrigues me, and I think he really could be invaluable in the future, especially if we want to expand our borders. He really has a knack for turning bad situations around and making everyone feel like they got what they wanted. The only person he was not successful with in this endeavor was me.

Prince Charles fit nicely in between all the other princes. His kingdom of Marcynth was in the northeast. His kingdom was making strides with forging alliances with the kingdoms in the far north, and could be a real benefit to our land if this proved to work itself out. He had curly brown hair and chocolate colored eyes that made you feel at home. He was well-built in the muscle department, had full lips, and an easy smile for his friends. He was going to turn seventeen years at the time of the sun's zenith, just a few moon cycles before I turn twenty. His easy going nature made him fun to be around most of the time, but I was concerned he lacked the discipline to rule a kingdom, at least at this point. He could be petty upon occasion as well, and I found this trait rather irksome.

Prince Kalvin was my "least" favorite. Do not get me wrong, he was easy to look at. He just had the expectation that I should come to him and that he should not have to come to me. Maybe he was right. It was unfair, but a girl should not be the one to pursue a man. Kalvin was about to turn seventeen in a couple of moon cycles. He had blonde hair and blue eyes like me. He was well-toned, and had an athletic build. He was very agile and quick. He reminded me of a cat that could silently stalk its prey and strike without them even knowing he was there. This made me slightly apprehensive around him. His kingdom, Heraldin, was the most strategic of the six kingdoms, being in the center. His kingdom was the hub around which we all dispersed. From a logical standpoint, it would make the most sense for me to choose Kalvin, but I knew I would always feel a bit jumpy around him.

I often wondered if any prince would really want me, if it was not for this whole bonded thing. I was short, only five feet four inches, slender, and I was not beautiful like the queens of the other kingdoms. I was pretty, and everyone commented that my bright blue eyes were my best feature. My eyes were rimmed with long lashes that seemed to encourage people to talk and share things with me they normally would have kept to themselves. I guess I just had one of those trusting natures that people connected with. I found it difficult at times to listen to their stories of heartbreak. My heart would ache along with theirs, and often they brought tears to my eyes. I knew that this was not a good trait for a future queen, as we were to be stoic, yet pleasant. We were expected to endure whatever the king demanded of us, and do it with a pleasant attitude. I always found this impossible. I always found myself arriving at anger quickly, and I could never hide it. Everyone always knew exactly what I was feeling. I just could not shut it off.

A rumbling started under my feet. It felt like a tickle, and made me feel a bit disorientated, but it stopped quickly enough. I had never felt anything like it, and I went to inquire what was happening.

¥

"Mother, what was that rumble in the ground just a few minutes ago?" My mother, Amanda, was in her room as always. With the entire castle to roam around in, I never understood why she always stayed confined to her room unless duty called her elsewhere.

"My darling girl, do not worry. It was just an earthquake. We have not had any of those since you were a baby. They are usually small and nothing to be concerned about."
"Mother, were you nervous when you married my father?"
"Yes, very much so, I am afraid to admit. Your father was a large man, at six foot three inches, and I am a foot shorter than him. When I first met him my eyes widened to the size of saucers in disbelief that I would be enough to satisfy a man like that, especially since I was just a year past my first blood flow. I think it was my large blue eyes and blonde hair that attracted him to me. I certainly was not strong or confident. In fact, I was the ideal description of what a female should be. I think your father liked the fact that he could control me. Maybe that was the real reason he chose me after all. He had such strongly defined facial features, and it always made

him appear hard and unyielding. I guess when ruling a kingdom, this is an asset. It just left me terrified."

"In a way, I was happy about the curse. Do not ever breathe a word of this to anyone, Annaliessa, do you understand?"

"Yes, Mother, please continue."

"I was glad I would only have to bear one child. After the initial attempts at trying for a second child once the curse had been placed on the land, he seldom came to my bed at all. I stay to my room so as to not remind him I am around and that he can lay claim to his marital rights any time he chooses. I do not care if he is sharing a bed with another woman, as long as it is not mine. It keeps me happier this way."

"Mother, is sharing a bed with a man that horrible? Am I going to have to look forward to my marriage night with dread, and not anticipation?"

"My dear, if you marry for love, and not obligation, I am sure you will not suffer the same fate as me. I am sure one of the princes has to have captured your attention by now. I personally have always thought that you and Jordan would make the best match."

"Why do you say that?"

"My dear, do you not see the way he looks at you?"

"That is just the bonding, mother. I would not put to much stock in a look." My mother laughed.

"What is so humorous?"

"The bonding portion of the curse did not start until each of you reached the point of physical development that typical transpires just after you leave childhood behind. I remember the day of your first blood flow, you were horrified, as most girls are; knowing they are eligible for marriage at any point after that. Until that time, you were operating under complete free will."

"I still do not see your point."

"Annaliessa, Jordan has been looking at you like you were an angel sent from heaven since you were in your ninth year. Well before either of you had left the childhood stage."

"Is there anything else that makes you think we make a good match?"

"Jordan is a smart young man. He is generous, fair, confident, and he seems to be quite the romantic. The fact that he is extremely handsome and well-built does not hurt either."

"Hmm. What makes you say romantic?"

"Ever since that sun's zenith time, when you were nine years and he was a boy of eight years, he has been claiming that one day you would be his wife, you would not be subject to the curse, and that you would bless him with many children. He has never paid attention to any other girl or woman, and he has never made such a claim about anyone else. When he looks at you, it is with the look of a man in love, like there is no one else in the room but you. I am sure he would be a very sensitive and attentive lover."

"Mother! Please do not talk to me about what he would be like in bed. I am trying not to think about the marital obligations I will have to fulfill. In fact, the only couple I have ever seen that seems to be enamored with each other is Jordan's parents, King Nicholas and Queen Sarah. I have always hoped that the man I marry would be like that. He is always with her, he holds her hand when he thinks no one is looking, and I catch them smiling and sharing knowing glances with each other all the time. I want that, and I should be able to have it."

"Of course, you should. I hope that you will have everything I never had. I must say, if that is what you want, then your best chance of obtaining it is with Jordan. He has seen the way his father treats his mother, and I am sure he will treat his wife in a like manner; well, assuming that person is you. If he is forced to marry someone out of obligation, then I would have to guess he will fulfill his duties and nothing more."

"Mother, why is it you would rather my father share a bed with another woman? I cannot imagine having my husband bedding another woman and being agreeable to it."

"Your father, like I said, is more interested in control, than he is in making anyone else happy. He was always forceful in taking what he wanted from me, and it was quite unpleasant, especially the first time. I cried all night from the pain. The second time was not as painful, but he was still uncaring and brutal in taking what he felt entitled to. I always felt so empty after he got up and left the room. I tried to focus on what my child would look like, given that your father has brown hair and eyes, and I with blonde hair and blue eyes. I had hoped you would get my fairer features, since his father had a fairer coloring as well. Luckily, something good came out of it, and I did have the fairer featured child I was praying for."

"So you see, daughter, those other women are saving me from having to endure a rather unpleasant event, and for that I am actually grateful."

"Thank you for speaking with me so openly, mother. You have given me enough to think upon for now. I will take my leave and let you get some rest. Mother, I love you. I hope you know that."

"I do. I love you more than you can imagine, Annaliessa. Good-bye, my darling one."

Bondage Breaker

3

I lay in my bed that night, wishing there was some way to end the bond between the princes so I could be sure of my own feelings as well as theirs.

This was insane. I did not need a man to love me to feel complete. I was quite happy just the way I was. I wanted to wait until I felt ready to marry and that I was sure I loved my future husband without reservation. I wanted my wedding night to be something special, not something I had to look forward to with dread.

"I love myself! I do not need a man to make me feel loved! I am a strong and smart woman, and I do not need a man to protect me or to make decisions for me! Do you hear me, whoever you are, that put this curse and bond on me and our families? I love myself just the way I am, and I am not going to marry because you have bound me to someone I have no choice with!" I screamed this into the darkness, and lay back spent and exhausted. I hoped I did not wake anyone else in the castle with my screams. I was just so angry. I was still shaking with it when I felt a breeze move through my room.

I heard the sound of distant laughter, and then I heard the faint whisper, "You are released of your bond and those that are bound to you are also free, princess. You still bear the curse, and since you can only marry nobility, you will suffer the same fate as your parents, one child. Choose well pretty one, your destiny and those of the surrounding kingdoms lie in your hands."

The air went still, and I somehow felt lighter, as if a weight had been removed from me. I knew something significant had taken place, and I could not wait to find out if the princes had felt the change as well.

¥

At the same moment, in the kingdom of Vulterrian, Jordan sat bolt upright in bed. He felt as if someone had removed a chain from around his neck, but was not sure what it meant. He knew without a doubt that he needed to talk to Annaliessa immediately. He would set out on the journey first thing in the morning.

¥

I would eventually find out that the same thing was taking place with the other princes that night.

Within six days, all of the princes would be in Petroset, expecting to have their questions answered. No one was prepared for what actually happened.

Day of Reckoning

4

I was awoken early the next morning by my bed shaking violently. I jumped out of bed and grabbed a simple dress to go over my undergarments as I rushed from my room. People were scattering in every direction with sheer panic etched on their faces. I grabbed one of the servant men as he hurried past and asked him what was happening.

"Earthquake, the worst I have ever felt. It is not safe to stay; the mountain might give way and crush the castle. You must flee right away, Princess. Do not stop for anything! Just run as fast as you can to the villages outside the castle walls."

I released the strangle-hold I had on the man's arm and ran to my mother's room. It was empty. My mother had already gotten out of the castle at least that is what I hoped. I did not care if my father lived or died, so I started to make my way to the stairway that would lead me to the outer courtyard. The stones and wooden support beams started to split and I knew I only had a few moments to get out or risk being trapped. I saw a small child, one of the servant's I was sure, scared and huddled into a ball by a door crying. I ran to her, and told her to give me her hand. She was so distraught she did not even register that I was there. I went to pick her up, but she fought me, pummeling me with her small fists, crying "Wait for mommy! Wait for mommy!"

I knew the journey down the already weakened staircase was going to be challenging enough without adding a thrashing child to the equation, but I had no choice. I could not leave her.

I stumbled forward and tried to make the first step, but the shaking of the earth was so intense, that I lost my footing, and fell backwards. I lost my grip on the toddler, and she jumped out of my arms and began to run back to the bedroom. I saw the first beam completely split in two, and I knew I could not go back if I was going to make it down the stairs before it collapsed. I dragged my aching body off the ground and held onto the side wall for as much support as it could provide, which at this point was very little. I made my way down the stairs as I heard the rumbling and deafening groan of timber and rocks giving way on the upper staircase. I bolted for the door, and managed to beat the cloud of suffocating dust from the collapsing staircase. I made my way to the courtyard and found it almost deserted. I thought about running for the stables to see if there was a horse I could ride, but thought better of it, as they were likely already gone. I had no choice but to propel myself forward and get as far away from the castle as I could.

I broke through the outer wall of the courtyard and knew that the village was still at best a mile away. I was not sure how I was going to make it, as my legs and back hurt from my fall on the stairs, and my lungs felt like they were on fire from the half-mile I had already run through the courtyard. I just needed to take a minute to catch my breath. That is when I heard what sounded like thunder cracking in the distance. I turned to look back and I saw an avalanche of rock, dirt, and trees crashing down toward the castle. I knew at that moment that the home I was born and raised in would not stand another day.

I was so captured by the sight of the avalanche that I did not see the ground begin to pull apart and I fell about six feet down into a crevice. Thankfully, it did not split further, and I managed to grab some roots, and found a small foothold for my feet. I knew in my already weakened state, I could not hold on forever.

Just when I thought I was about to spend my last moments alive, I saw the face of a young man peer over the crevice. I thought I heard the cry of a baby in the distance, but it was hard to be sure of anything with the noise of the avalanche which sounded as if it was almost on top of the castle at this point.

"Grab my hands!" shouted the young man. I grabbed on, but I knew I did not have the strength to hold tight for long. Thankfully, he was quite strong, and pulled me effortlessly out of the crevice. He then picked up a small bundle, an infant, and grabbed my hand and yelled, "Run!"

We were no match for the literal mountain of debris crashing onto my home. The courtyard would capture and contain some of the debris, but it was building so fast I knew it would spill over the stone walls of the courtyard and overtake us. I could barely manage to run in my condition, and he was slowed due to having to cradle an infant. I once again braced myself mentally for the fact that this might be the moment of my death.

I heard an unearthly roar from above and almost fainted in disbelief as the dragon swooped down and landed a few hundred feet ahead of us. I could hear his voice in my mind tell me to climb on, that he was here to save me. I was not sure if he could read my mind as well, but the only thing screaming through it was, *There is no way in Hades I am getting on top of a dragon.* I hate heights, especially the kind that move.

He was a shimmering blue-green, like running water catching the rays of the sun. There were feathers from the crown of his forehead to his mid-back where they spread out over his wings. His tail was full of spikes that looked fatal to anything that crossed its projected path. A lethal package, and yet, he was here to save me.

I guess he understood my thoughts as well, as he issued me another command to climb on, and that there was no time for me to argue. I was frozen there in front of this legendary creature. The young man stood there looking confused, so he obviously was not hearing the dragon's thoughts as I was.

I must have stood there frozen and dazed for too long, as the dragon began to flap his wings and lift from the ground. I closed my eyes and felt tears running down my cheeks as I realized my stupidity and fear was going to cause our death. I did not have this thought long, as I felt claws enclose themselves around me and my feet left the earth. My tears turned to screams, and I kept my eyes tightly closed. I did not want to look down to my impending doom should this creature find me more trouble than I was worth, nor could I look to see my home completely destroyed by the forces of nature.

In just a few minutes, we were dropped carefully onto a grassy field, and the dragon landed a few feet away.

I was feeling a little foolish for my behavior, and very, very thankful, to a creature I thought was just a story told to scare children into minding their parents.

In my mind I asked, *"What is your name, dragon?"*

"My name is Evirent and I have been guardian to your Kingdom for eighty and seven years now."

"Why have I never seen or heard about you?"

"You have never had need of my services until now."

"Do you protect all the kingdoms and all the royals, or just particular ones?"

"We look after those that are pure in heart, and not bent on the evil inclinations of man."

"So, if my father had been in danger as I was, you would not have saved him?"

"No."

"How is it I can hear you speak to my mind?"

"Dragons are mystical creatures. We carry a special kind of magic, but only intervene when we see an injustice, such as your death would have brought."

"So are there more of you?"

"Yes, but not as many as we once were. Our birth rates coincide with yours in this land, and the curse has left our numbers dwindling as well, since we only have one mate for life. Men; wanting to make a name for themselves, have been hunting us down for trophies, and your father was the man behind my mate's death. If it were not for the fact that we live to be several hundred years old, we would be extinct."

"So my life is important to yours somehow?"

"Your life is important to a great many people."

"How so?"

"That, young one is not for you to know just yet. You will understand in due time. Right now you and this young man need to find shelter in the village."

Since this entire exchange happened in my mind, the young man just kept staring at me and then back at the dragon. I think he thought I was crazy, or maybe he was questioning his own sanity.

"What is your name?" I asked the young man.

"I am Tyson."

"Is the infant yours?"

"No, its mother had fallen and hit her head while fleeing and was dead when I found her. I could not leave a helpless infant behind, so I picked it up and as I was running out of the courtyard walls, I saw the ground swallow you up."

"Thank-you, Tyson, for saving me from the crevice. It appears I owe you and a dragon a deep debt of gratitude."

The dragon gave what looked like a nod, and started to lift off the ground.

I yelled after Evirent, "Wait! Will I ever see you again?"

"Should you ever need me in a time of crisis, you just have to call my name and say that you need me, and I will get there as quickly as I can," he said in a voice that sounded like trees cracking and falling to the ground.

I can see why they prefer the mental form of communication, as his voice was terrifying. "How will you know where I am?" I called out after him.

"I always know where you are." With that, he flew away.

I looked at Tyson and said, "I guess we better get to the village and find a place to stay."

"You have not told me your name yet," Tyson stated.

It was my chance to experience life outside the confines of the castle and my destiny, but that would be impossible if anyone knew who I really was, so giving my real name was out of the question. "You can call me Anna."

"Do you have any family that was able to escape the castle?" I asked.

"No, my mother died last year. I never knew my father, and I was the only child. What about you?"

"Yes, I will eventually find my mother and father, as we were separated during our escape. I will just have to find which village they have sought refuge in."

"Will they be worried about you?"

"I imagine my mother will be frantic with worry about my well-being. I am not sure if my father will be quite as distraught. After all, I am only a girl."

I knew I must have looked quite frightful at the moment, and I was not dressed regally at all, but I could not understand why Tyson was unable to recognize me.

"Tell me, how are you able to communicate with dragons, and why one would be inclined to save you?"

"Well, I honestly do not know. Until today, I did not even know they really existed. It has been a very unusual day, and I am still trying to figure it all out."

We fell silent for the few minutes walk to the village. I noted that Tyson was the first man I was ever going to be alone with for what may be longer than a few minutes. I felt an unusual fluttering sensation in my stomach whenever I felt bold enough to glance his way. He was tall, at least six feet two inches, with shoulder length black hair that had a bit of a wave to it, and stunning green eyes. He was well-built, strong, and had very full, kissable lips. *What on earth was I thinking? Where did 'kissable' come from?*

The way he cradled the infant in his arms made my heart melt. Not only did he put his own life on the line for this babe that was not even his, but he even stopped to help save me. He was a good man from what I had seen so far. *I hope he does not disappoint me later and turn into a self-absorbed egotistical piece of flesh, destined to bestow on us women-kind his favor by gracing us with glances, or entering into idle conversation, as many carry themselves about. This is my one chance to fall in love for real, and I want to take it. I am in no hurry to locate my father, and if Tyson does not recognize me as the princess, I am going to take advantage of however long I have, before reality comes back to haunt me.*

Grace

5

As we neared the village, Tyson got closer to me and asked me to hold the baby. He said he wanted us to look like any normal couple, as it would make it easier to find a place to stay.

I had no trouble accommodating his request. In fact, I found his closeness to be somewhat intoxicating. As we got to the village inn, he put his arm around my waist and whispered, "Stay close, and let me do the talking."

We walked into the bustling inn, and approached the bar. Tyson waved over a young woman and inquired as to whether or not they still had a room. I saw the girl look Tyson over appraisingly, and then give me a scowl.

"Sorry there, handsome, but as you can see, we have more than we can handle as it is."

"Is there a place where my family and I can find a place to sleep for the night?"

"Let me ask a few of the village elders that are here. Just give me a few minutes."

"If looks were deadly, I think I would have been inflicted with a fatal wound," I said in a whisper.

"What are you talking about?" Tyson asked.

"That bar maid. Did you see the way she looked at you? Like you were the last chicken leg during a famine, and then gave me a look that said she would be happy to watch me starve to death."

"Sorry, I really did not notice. Besides, I would make sure you got the chicken leg before she did."

I was not prone to blushing, but at that moment, I am certain I turned a brilliant shade of pink if the heat in my cheeks was any indication. I tried to look down and pretend I was checking on the baby, but he saw it, and I saw a small smile form on his lips.

The bar maid made her way back over to us, and without acknowledging I was even there, she told Tyson of a young couple that just lost their baby and would most likely be sympathetic to us. If I was not mistaken, she was going out of her way to accentuate her womanly figure to Tyson. I felt anger begin to prick the surface, and I again, had to check myself. *What is wrong with me? He doesn't belong to me, so why am I acting and feeling like he does?* I bit the inside of my lip to bring myself under control. I had a very strong urge to reach out and strike her, but remembered I was playing the part of a tired, new mother, and I did not want to ruin the provision Tyson had managed to obtain.

Tyson listened as she gave directions to the home of Joseph and Maria on the outskirts of the village. She gave me one more look, as if she was trying to place my face but could not quite get it. Tyson thanked her, and we turned and left the inn.

"You did a great job of being a tired and doting mother. If everything works out, I am hoping I can leave the infant with this couple. Since her child just died two days ago, she may even be able to nurse this baby."

"Are you going to pretend you are my husband when we get to the house?"

"No, I think it will make it easier to leave the infant with the couple, if they do not see us as potential parent material."

"So what exactly will be our relationship?" I queried.

"Just unrelated survivors of the earthquake that helped each other get to safety. Since you are an unmarried woman, I cannot leave you alone and unprotected, so until your family is located, I am looking out for your well-being."

"That seems like a reasonable approach. Tell me, Tyson, how many years are you?"

"I am now twenty and three years."

"How did your mother die?"

"She died defending me while seeking justice."

"That seems like a short answer for a very long story. One I hope you will tell me one day."

"I would not get your hopes up. That is not a story I easily share."

We rounded a corner and saw the house the bar maid described in front of us. Tyson knocked on the door, and we heard voices on the other side questioning who could possibly be visiting today of all days.

The door was opened by a stocky, not fat, man of average height, with black, shoulder length, straight hair and sad brown eyes. "May I help you?"

"We stopped at the inn and they told us you may be willing to take us in for at least the night. We have a small infant that we rescued from the earthquake, and we are looking for a couple that might give it a loving home."

"The infant is not yours?"

"No sir. In fact, we were strangers until just an hour ago."

"Tyson saved the baby and then me during the earthquake. He will not let me go off alone since I am just a young woman with no other protection. He has agreed to look after me until I can locate my family."

"Please, you must be exhausted. Come in. Have a seat at the table and I will get my wife, Maria."

We offered our thanks as we entered and sank down into the chair. They were simple wooden chairs, but to my aching body, they felt like a silk cushion.

A petite, red-haired women with enchanting green eyes, and a sweet, likeable face came rushing out of the room to the right of the fireplace.

"Welcome. My name is Maria. And you are?"

"I am Tyson, and this is Anna."

"What is the baby's name?"

"The baby is not ours. We rescued it, and are hoping you will want to raise it as your own," Tyson said expectantly.

"May I hold it? Is it a boy or a girl?"

"I do not know. I did not look to see."

Maria took the infant from my arms and stared lovingly down into its face. She began to unwrap the blanket and saw that the child was in need of changing. She excused herself and went into the other room to attend to the infant. The cries of the baby started, most likely as soon as she removed the cloth. I am sure the poor thing was starving as well.

"Can I get you a little something to eat and drink?" asked Joseph.

"Yes, please!" was the simultaneous response from both Tyson and I.

By the time we finished the bread and fruit, Maria had come back into the main room of the house.

"It is a girl. I think we will call her Tabitha, if that is alright with you two."

"It is fine," both Tyson and I stated in unison again. "It is a lovely name," I added.

"Is there a place where we can relieve ourselves and perhaps clean up a bit?" I asked quietly.

"Certainly, you must be feeling rather dusty from the travel. I will fill up a pitcher of water and you can take turns washing in the other room to the left of the fireplace. I think I have a simple house dress that you can change into, Anna. Joseph will give you the other instructions, including where you will each sleep. I am going to retire, as I am sure I will be up a few times through the night to feed the baby."

Tyson allowed me to clean up first. I was never so grateful for a bowl of water and a cloth. Maria even let me use her hair brush. My hair was full of tangles, and I just could not manage it on my own. Perhaps tomorrow I could ask her to help me get the worst of them out.

I sat by the fire as Tyson took the opportunity to clean up. Joseph came in with a bundle of straw. "This is for you to sleep on. Once Tyson is finished in the other room, I will lay this down for you to make your bed on. Tyson can sleep on the floor by the fire."

"If you do not mind, I would like to sleep by the fire, as I tend to get cold during the night time."

"I cannot put the straw down for you by the fire. Surely, you would rather be a bit chilled but comfortable?"

Tyson caught the last sentence, and inquired about what Joseph meant.

"She would rather sleep on the floor in front of the fire to stay warm, than sleep on the straw and be comfortable in the other room."

"He is right. You should take the bed of straw in the bedroom. It is better for me to sleep on the floor."

"Right or not, I cannot sleep when I am cold, so I will get more sleep on the floor in front of the fire, than I will on a bed of straw where I am cold."

"Alright, but if you find you want to switch during the middle of the night, do not say we did not warn you of your folly."

Joseph gave us each a blanket and a bundle of rags to use as a pillow. After saying goodnight, he joined his wife in the other room.

Tyson offered me one last chance to change my mind before saying goodnight and exiting to the bedroom.

I decided to take my dress off and use it to separate me from the floor. Besides, I did not feel as if I would be comfortable sleeping in it, as I was accustomed to sleeping in my undergarments. *I hope I will be the first to rise in the morning, so as not to embarrass myself by being immodest in my lack of proper attire.*

I was exhausted and found myself drifting off to sleep immediately.

Connections

6

I could not have been asleep for more than a few hours when I felt something nudging my fingers. I thought I was dreaming, but then I felt little razor-sharp teeth take a nibble on my little finger. I awoke instantly, and tried to stifle the shriek I instinctively made. I was able to cut it off as my surroundings reminded me that I was not in my large stone room at the castle, and any sound I made would awaken everyone. I knew I would not endear myself to our benefactors if I managed to wake the baby before it was ready to feed. I think the mouse was more afraid of my sudden movement, than I was, and it scurried off to find a safe place to hide.

I was getting ready to inspect my wound when I heard moaning coming from the room Tyson was sleeping in. I got up and tip-toed to the door, pressing my ear against it. I heard what sounded like the crying plea of a little boy, not that of a man. *"Please stop! I'll be good. I promise! Give me another chance, please!"*

I decided to open the door and peek inside. The oil lamp was still burning, so I could see Tyson squirming around in the straw, whimpering. The blanket had fallen to his waist, and my eyes were drawn to his muscle-defined midsection. I cannot say what my fascination was with the male body as of late, but it certainly was causing me some distress lately. I felt a blush reach my cheeks and I decided it was better if I just focused on his face. He had such a look of pain furrowed onto his countenance, that it gripped my heart fiercely. I wanted to take him in my arms and tell him it would be alright, but I dared not entertain such a scandalous idea. After all, I was in my undergarments. *What would happen if someone even caught me staring at him now?* It seemed as if the nightmare was ebbing away, and he was settling into a deeper sleep. I felt that it was best for me to find my way back to my own sleeping spot, but I was not sure if sleep was going to be within my grasp for the rest of the night. I stepped back and closed the door. I turned to make my way back to the fireplace and thought I should wash my finger where the mouse had bitten me. The problem was, I only knew one place that had water, and it was in the room with Tyson.

He did seem like he was deeply asleep, so I thought I could sneak in and get the pitcher without being detected. *Stupid mouse! Why did it have to nibble on me? Maybe the straw bed would have been best.*

I crept back to the door and slowly opened it enough for me to pass through. I kept myself close to the wall as I made my way to the table the water pitcher was on. I glanced over my shoulder to make sure Tyson was still sleeping. Unfortunately, in so doing, I gauged the distance to the table wrong, and found myself bumping into it. The pitcher began to wobble and I shot out my hand to steady it, but it was too late. Tyson sat up and said, "What are you doing in..., w-w-where is your dress?"

It is a good thing it was dark by the table, with just the dim glow from the single oil lamp, so he could not see the look of mortification on my face, nor the bright red shade my whole body must be turning. "I was bitten by a mouse and this was the only place I knew to find water to wash the bite. I did not mean to wake you and cause such a show of immodesty," I whispered, without turning to look at him.

He said, "Do not turn around, so I can put my pants on. I will come and take a look at the bite. You are right to wash it. You do not want to risk the wound festering."

Do not turn around? Was he joking? I was glued to this spot from embarrassment. I also felt my heart beating so wildly in my chest that I was sure he could hear it across the room. *Calm down,* I kept repeating in my mind. *He is just going to look at the bite. I am making too much out of this. He is not going to be focusing on what you are not wearing, just your finger. Besides, it is dark enough that he is not going to see much of anything.* Well, it was the lie I had to tell myself to keep from shaking as he approached.

I felt his presence close the gap and without turning, stuck my hand out to keep him from getting any closer. I still had my dignity after all.

He had the oil lamp in one hand, and with the other took the hand I had proffered for inspection. The warmth from his hand did little to ease my nervousness. My hand was feeling tingly all over, sending spark-like sensations up my arm. I shifted my footing to hide the shiver that was making its way through my body.

"It broke through your skin, and it is bleeding slightly. It definitely needs to be cleaned with some water. Tomorrow I will look for some herbs and roots that I can use to make a salve for it, to keep the chance of infection to a minimum."

"You are a healer? What if the mouse was a carrier of the plague, or worse, the 'crazies' and I go mad in a couple of days, and some one has to kill me before I harm anyone else?"

"You have such an active imagination, Anna. I am surprised you are able to fall asleep at all at night with thoughts like that going through your head."

"Well, it is true. It can happen. I have heard the stories. Even the most timid of persons can become crazed killers after being bitten by a rat or mouse carrying that disease."

"I think the herbs and roots will be sufficient."

I turned my head so that I looked directly at him. "I have heard that some of the healers also know magic. Have you acquired this skill?"

"I have learned a few things over the years, but magic is not something to play with Anna, and it is not something to be used for your amusement. It can have serious repercussions."

"So you do know some magic! Are you worried you could accidentally turn me into a frog?" I said jokingly, trying to lighten the tension I could feel building in the space between us.

"You have been listening to way too many children's stories. Not everything has a happy ending, you know."

A look of pain fleeted across his face, and I felt my heart flip at the thought of him in pain. "So is that why you have nightmares? You have never experienced a happy ending?"

"Nightmare? Were you spying on me?"

"No, I heard you when the mouse awakened me with its bite."

"What exactly did you hear?"

"You crying for someone to give you another chance and asking them to stop doing whatever it was they were doing in your dream."

He sucked in a deep breath, and said, "Perhaps if I was as fortunate as one of the princes and had the freedoms and power they wield, I could gain a happy ending much more easily. Some of us do not get everything handed to us on a silver platter, but we have to toil for it everyday. Surely you understand this, do you not?"

I was one of the royals he spoke of, but if he thought my life was a bed of roses, he was sadly mistaken. I really could not say anything, however, or I would risk giving my identity away.

"I understand that happy endings are harder to come by than anyone might think. That does not explain the nightmare I overheard a few moments ago. That was much more than just not having a happy ending. What happened to you to cause you so much pain and sadness that you carry it around with you even when you sleep?"

"You should mind your own business, and worry less about things that are not your concern."

"I only ask, because I have found that it sometimes helps if you can share it with someone else. If you do not want to tell me, you are free to hang on to your secrets. We all have secrets, Tyson. Some are easier to share than others, but a heart burdened with pain only leads to destruction. I have found forgiveness a very worthwhile release, yet there are some I, too, struggle to forgive. I wish it were not so, as I think anger and hate bring about far worse things to someone's heart and soul than we realize. However, there are some hurts that are tougher to let go of, and I am still working on these myself. So I guess I cannot judge you if you are suffering to do the same."

"I cannot imagine anyone wanting to hurt you, Anna. Who has caused your kind heart such injury?"

"That, Tyson, will be my secret for now. What about that magic?"

"Changing the topic of conversation I see. It is always easier to ask someone else to bare their soul than to unburden your own."

"Fine! In the interest of extending the proverbial olive branch, I will tell you. It is my father. He is cruel and hard-hearted. He is quick to anger and thinks nothing of exercising his right to physical punishment. He seems to get real pleasure when he can exercise it with his own hands, and gets a gleam of satisfaction at the bruises he inflicts. So, you see, I am in no hurry to return to my father's household."

"Who is your father?"

"What does it matter? He is just another man who treats women like they are dirt to be spat upon. Why women are in such a hurry to marry is a mystery to me. The only thing you are trading is one hell for another."

"Not all men are like that."

"I really am getting a bit chilled. Can you please just take care of the bite so I can return to the fire?"

What he did next totally surprised me. He took my hand to his nude chest and placed it over his heart. I felt the strength of his heart as it beat a rhythmic tune under my palm. My eyes were riveted to his chest, and I could feel the warmth begin to envelope my body. *What in all the realm of man was going on?*

"Are you feeling warmer now?"

"Yes, how are you doing that?"

"Another secret I am not going to tell you. Close your eyes and concentrate on your hand. Think about pushing all the bad diseases out of your body through that bite on your finger."

I gave him a skeptical look, but did as he had instructed. I felt him take my hand and put it between his hands. I was tempted to open my eyes just a crack when I felt him lift my hand up towards his face, but I did not want to risk ruining whatever he was doing. I felt him blow his warm breath onto my hand, like people do when it is cold outside. It sounded as if he was speaking an ancient language as he rubbed his hands over mine. I felt my body relaxing under his ministry, and it was as if he was caressing my very soul with every stroke of his hand. I suddenly wanted him to take me in his arms and hold me until the morning, and while I knew this would be wrong, the connection that had formed between us, felt perfectly natural. It was so peaceful and loving, something I could only dream about experiencing, and yet here in this moment, every hope I had ever held felt possible; within my reach. *Is this what it feels like to fall in love?* It was the last thought I had before unconsciousness overtook me.

New Experiences

7

I awoke with the sun streaming into the room. I was a bit disoriented at first, but then realized I was lying in the straw bed. My dress was draped over a small chest by the window. Tyson was not there. *What time is it, and how did I end up here?*

The last thing I remembered was the warmth of the connection that had touched my very soul as Tyson healed me. I brought my hand up for inspection and the wound was completely sealed. I kept staring at it in disbelief. The cry of a hungry baby brought me out of my own daydream-like state. I pulled the blanket from me and blushed as I realized Tyson must have laid me here, which means he got quite an eye full of me in my undergarments. I really am going to have to deal with sleeping in my dress for the next few days, as I cannot afford to be caught so exposed again. I quickly grabbed the dress and put it on so that I could offer some assistance to Maria.

I rushed out of the room and found Maria in a chair with Tabitha to her breast. Tyson must be outside somewhere for Maria to feel comfortable being so naked. Her complete chest was exposed, and I suddenly felt a bit self-conscious about my own development. It was not like I did not possess the alluring figure of a woman, but I could not help but feel a little inferior in that moment.

"What time is it Maria?"

"You must have had quite the trouble sleeping, as I see you ended up switching places with Tyson, and now it is well into the morn, almost time for the men to come in for breakfast. Do you know how to cook, Anna?"

"No, it was not a chore I was assigned in my house, at least not yet."

"Very well, Tabitha should be finished with her feeding in a few minutes. Would you mind going and collecting the eggs from the chicken pen out back? There is a basket by the door to put the eggs in."

"Sure, I think I can manage that."

I grabbed the basket and headed out the door to do my task. *I have never done any kind of chores before, but how hard could it be to pick up a few eggs?*

I found chickens can be a real mean bunch when they set their mind to it. I certainly did not have the temperament that soothed them, and found that there are worse things than a mouse bite.

I was literally chased from the chicken pen by the three hens. I fled as if my life depended on it, and hoped that the nine eggs I had managed to extract from the hens hiding spots would be enough for breakfast.

Of course, both Tyson and Joseph were present to witness my flight, and were both doubled over, laughing hysterically at me. I glowered at them, and shoved my way right between them on my way back into the house.

I put the eggs down onto the table and Maria handed me Tabitha while she redressed herself. "Anna, can you burp Tabitha while I get breakfast started? After that, would you be kind enough to set the plates and cups on the table? I will have everything ready shortly."

The men came in with a bucket of goat's milk and a bundle of wood for the fire. Joseph knelt behind Maria as she was working on our meal in front of the fire, and put his arms around her waist and planted a kiss on the spot where her neck meets her shoulder. She let out a small giggle and smiled appreciatively at him.

He asked if he could take Tabitha from me, and I obliged. I had to set the table anyway. Tyson's eyes followed my every movement. There was a hypnotizing hunger about his look, and it made me a little wary, but inquisitive all the same.

Maria instructed the men to wash up. I told her I would hold Tabitha while she ate her food first. She tried to fight me over it not being right since I was a guest, but I insisted. She seemed to be pleased by my small gesture, and happily partook of her meal.

When she was finished, I ate my meal and then asked if I could help wash up. She showed me where the basin was and how to draw water from the well and put it on the fire to warm a bit. I then washed my first set of dirty dishes. I was surprised at the sense of accomplishment I felt in this task that would be considered menial in my family.

Tabitha had gone back to sleep and I asked Maria if she would brush the tangles out of my hair. She seemed overjoyed at being able to do this, and I could not help but ask her why. "Maria, you seem so happy to be able to brush my hair. Why?"

"I remember my mother brushing my hair when I was growing up, and when you move away, you discover how much those times meant to you. My mother always told me stories, or we talked about things going on in the village. I remember the day I told her I saw Joseph and knew that he was the one I was going to give my heart to. So, doing it now for you makes all those wonderful times come rushing into the present, and remind me of how much I am looking forward to creating a similar time with Tabitha."

"Your mother brushes your hair, does she not?"

"Yes, but she does not talk like your mother did with you," I lied. I had a maid who did that task, and it was not soothing or pleasant like what I was encountering with Maria.

Tyson had come back into the house and stated that he was going to go hunting for some herbs and roots that he could find just outside the village. "Can I come with you?" I asked expectantly. "I have never been out exploring for such things, and I would really like to learn something about nature."

"I do not think it is proper, nor a prudent thing for the two of you to be out in the woods alone together," stated Maria. "However, I cannot deny that being cooped up inside all day would not be beneficial to your learning. Please promise that you will not stray too far into the woods and will be gone for no more than a couple of hours so that I do not worry myself too much about your safety."

"We will not stray too far, or be gone too long, will we Tyson?"

"Seeing as how I have a novice along on my quest, I am sure I will not be able to get too far out, as to cause any trouble. I assure you, we will return safe and sound in a couple of hours."

Tyson grabbed a leather pouch and slung it over his shoulder, and off we went.

Exploration and Provocation

8

The first hour of our trek out into the woods was exhilarating. I had never felt so free, and I was relishing every moment as if it were the last I might ever have. The reality was it might be. It was only a matter of time before my father located me. I was purposely going to stay out of the village proper so as to avoid recognition, and so far, none of my new acquaintances had made the connection to who I really was. *Was it the fact that my hair was not put up and my garments were plain that was causing them to accept me as Anna, a commoner?*

"Tyson, what do you dream about doing in the future, if you had the opportunity?"

"There is really only one thing I think about most days, and it is not something tender ears should be privy to."

"I am not naïve to the desires of the realm, or the wiles of men, Tyson. I think I can handle whatever you have to say."

"You think you can, but often once truth unveils the depravity of the mind, you will find you wish you remained unenlightened. I think the easier conversation is for you to tell me what a fair-haired maiden dreams of doing."

"I see. Am I always the one to expose my heart, and yet you wish for yours to remain a mystery? I think it is your turn to share, as I already told you one of my secrets last night."

He seemed to be contemplating what he should reveal, based on how he was studying my face. I had seen how men look at women when they are attracted to them, and it was the same look I saw reflected in his face. However, he seemed to be fighting something at the same time, and I was not sure if it was his feelings or something else.

He shook his head and seemed to relax a bit, as if he had come to a decision, but was mentally still piecing together what to say.

"I think this discussion is best if we recline under the shelter of a tree," Tyson said at last.

We found shelter under a large willow tree where the branches were so low it provided a screen from the path we were standing on moments ago, and wrapped us up into its secret place; one where lovers could exchange kisses and words of ardor without prying eyes to see. I would not normally agree to accompany a man into such a place where compromises of the gravest kind could be taken, but I just could not deny this man of what he requested.

"I am really unsure where to begin, but I will do my best. I was not a very bright child. Reading was a struggle for me. I could memorize anything if I heard it, but reading letters never quite worked for me. My teacher decided I was not trying hard enough and made me stay after class to work on this problem of mine. He was an evil man, and punished me so severely that it has left me with nightmares to this day. That is what you overheard last night."

"What did he do that would still trouble you so as a man?"

"Like I said, there are things that are not proper for a woman to hear, and I will not tell you the horror that men are capable of when they want to bend one to their will."

I knew all to well from my father what men were capable of, but I could tell this was the most he was going to reveal. My heart felt heavy in my chest. I wanted so much to reach out and take his pain. I did not realize I actually was reaching out my hand toward him until I felt my fingers touch his cheek.

The air became alive and felt tangible rather than invisible. I knew deep within me that something was transpiring between the two of us that neither one of us could stop. It was like the earthquake that caused the avalanche, no force in this land could have stopped it from continuing on its destructive course.

He reached out his hands and took my face between them and pulled me to his mouth. I immediately surrendered to his dominance and desire as he claimed my mouth and tongue in such a passionate way I could hardly remember to breathe. I did not want him to stop, I wanted to remain like this with him forever, but my life was not my own. *How could I expect to keep this man for myself, when I knew I must belong to another out of obligation? How is it possible that this young man could capture my heart so quickly?*

His kiss became less demanding and so tender just before he pulled away from me. I felt a sense of loss as he let go of my mouth, and could tell he felt it, too.

He continued to stare into my eyes, leaving me feeling vulnerable, yet secure all at the same time. There was still a bit of hardness to his eyes, which left me wondering what he was struggling with more, his past or his feelings for me. I was certain a man could not kiss a woman like that if he did not have feelings for her. Maybe I was being foolish, but I could not think of there being any other explanation. The real question that seemed to remain unanswered was whether or not my love was strong enough to heal his heart. I had to know if what he had just shared with me was special or if he made all the women he was with feel this way.

"Do you always bring women to hiding places such as this to seduce them?"

"Seduce you! What do you mean? I can assure you, I have not even begun to seduce you, nor would I. I have little use of the conventions men use for pleasure, and even less regard for the trappings of women," he said harshly.

I could not help but laugh at his harsh reply. He definitely was trying to hide his feelings, but why?
"What did I say that so amuses you?" he retorted.
"Your lips utter words that have little meaning. Your mouth betrays the truth. You can fool yourself, but you did not fool me. Your kiss was very persuasive in stating that the *trappings of women* are indeed something you crave, but want to deny, and I want to know why. Or is it just me in particular you want to toy with?"

"If I gave you the impression that a relationship is what I yearn for, I am most sorry. The fleeting impulses of women and the tedious nature of their whimsical sentiments are not of interest to me. Men are quite adept at making women believe they carry affection for them, but you would be wise not to react to such temptation. Once they have what they want, you will be of little consequence to them."

"It is a wonder women fall in love at all, if our fate is to be used solely for physical comfort, only to be tossed aside as a serious companion that can provide genuine fulfillment to a man in all aspect of their being. There is quite a difference in a dutiful wife and one who is devoted. If only men were intelligent enough to figure this out, our land would be a much happier and better place."

"You think I am stupid for being authentic in my beliefs and staunchly fulfilling my commitment to them? Is that not what the clerics declare from church pulpits every Sabbath; to be faithful and loyal to what you believe, and act in accordance to it?"

"When you are tired of lying to yourself, let me know, but I think I have had enough of nature for today." With that, I rose and headed back to the house.

Tyson stayed under the tree as I walked back to the house alone. I was not sure what exactly he was trying to hide from his past, but whatever it was, it was definitely affecting the present. *What had I gotten myself into now?* His explanation was not nearly detailed enough to explain the turmoil he seemed to be wrestling with, and I was beginning to wonder if it would become a barrier that was insurmountable in winning his heart completely. He certainly wanted me to think that way, based on his statement about *staunchly fulfilling my commitment. What commitment could he be referring too?*

¥

I sat alone under the tree wrestling internally with myself after Anna left. *Why now, after all these years without the need of anyone, let alone a woman, am I feeling as if I am falling in love, or at least that is what I am assuming this irrational sensation is? I have no room for this in my life. I owe it to my mother to carry out the revenge on King Claude she had started, and involving Anna would put her in jeopardy. It would not be beneath King Claude to torture and kill her if he found out how I felt about her, and I cannot risk the pain of that loss. I have no choice. I have to stay focused on my goal no matter how much of a challenge it will be. I will not let Anna play me like a fiddle. I am the master of my destiny, and I will just have to prove that to her, no matter how difficult that might be.*

Dreamweaver

9

The time for sleep had finally arrived. It was as if time had deliberately slowed down after my encounter under the willow tree with Tyson. He had spent most of the day pretending I was a mere annoyance that was to be tolerated. He was doing his best to divert his feelings, but I did not care. He could keep his fickle heart. I had no reason to collect useless artifacts that would gather dust on the shelf of regret. I had enough burdens, and another regret was just too heavy to carry.

I did not argue tonight about sleeping in the room with the straw. I was not keen on having another rendezvous with the mouse. Sleep eluded me for a long while, but I felt myself finally succumb to the sweet release it brings.

I am dreaming. I must be or how else would I hear a woman's voice whisper to me.

"Annaliessa, I bear the key to unlocking your curse," the voice called out to me.

This grabbed my attention and I whispered back to the voice in my dream, *"What key?"*

"The curse only applies if a royal marries another royal or nobility. You only have to marry someone not destined for a throne, someone other than nobility or of royal blood."

"If I marry someone like Tyson, I will not be cursed? Does this apply to the princes as well?" I queried.

"It applies to you all. You would do well to marry Tyson. He is in love with you, even if he will not admit it. Is that not what you wanted, to marry for love?"

I did not want the woman to go. I had so many questions, and yet I felt her presence fading away. "He loves me. You are certain?" I called out to her hoping she would answer me. There was only silence. *Who was this woman who kept speaking to me? Why did she care about the curse, and what connection did she have to Tyson that she would know his feelings as well? Could this be the witch my father had executed so long ago? Perhaps she is not dead after all, and we were only told she was executed. It would not be unlike my father to manufacture a lie if he was unsuccessful in an endeavor, just so he could save face.*

¥

I was wide awake and heard Anna ask, *He loves me. You are certain?* To whom she was speaking, I could not tell.

She must be dreaming. Was I in her dream? Did she love me? Was it possible? Was she referring to some other man in her dream, some one from the kingdom courtyard, where the more privileged of society dwelt? I hope it is me she is dreaming of, even though I know I should not harbor this wish if I am going to continue the path I have chosen. Maybe I could have both love and revenge. With that last prospect echoing in my mind, I found the sleep I desperately needed.

Intentions

10

I awoke with the cries of a baby just before sunrise. The few hours of sleep were going to play havoc on my determination to try to keep my feelings under wraps. I really had to see her and try and establish if I was the man in her dreams. I could not risk revealing my emotions unless I was certain she felt the same way toward me.

I heard Anna begin to stir in the other room, and felt my heart beat faster. I really was losing all sense of self-control, and normally this would unnerve me, but for some reason I was feeling giddy with the sense of abandon coursing through my veins.

Anna came out several minutes later looking even prettier than she did the day before, if that was even possible. She looked at me without the slightest hint of a smile, and headed for the back door without even as much as a courteous 'Good morning'.

She was obviously still holding a grudge against my actions and words of yesterday. *Why am I putting myself through this? Do I really need a woman to govern my sense of well-being and prove my self-worth? Oh, what a truly feeble resolve I possess! I hope I can carry out revenge better than I can withstand the advances of my emotions where Anna is concerned.*

I knew she had gone to collect the eggs, so I went to ascertain if I could gain access to the secret of her dream.

¥

I was in a vulnerable state this morning. The dream from last night plagued my mind and twisted my emotions like a grapevine winding its way around the support of a branch. How can I entice the truth from Tyson without being obvious in my attempt? He was so infuriating! I was going to prove that I was not some girl he could trifle with. He had met his match and I was no coward when it came to tackling the things that stood in my way. I was a fighter, and he was about to be blindsided with my wrath if he tried anything like yesterday. Being so focused on my anger, I did not realize he was leaning in the doorway watching me wrestle with the hens for their eggs. When I turned to the door, I about jumped out of my skin and had to regain myself before all the eggs ended up on the floor of the chicken pen.

"How long have you been standing there, and what do you want?" I said with as much coldness as possible.

"I think you have another secret you want to tell me," he said casually, but with the playfulness that suggested he thought he had the upper hand.

"I guess you should give me a hint, because I can assure you, there is nothing I am interested in sharing with you."

"It appears I am not the only one who talks in my sleep," Tyson said with a twinkle in his eyes.

"What is it you think you heard that has you testing my charity toward you today?"

"It appears that the honorable woman before me may not be as innocent as she wants people to believe."

"Now who is dreaming? Did you hit your head while you were rolling around on the floor last night? It seems that you have a very wild and vivid imagination, Tyson, and I have no desire to stoke the flames of that beast."

"Ouch! Some one is testy this morning. Did your lover turn you away in your dream, and so you feel the need to exact revenge on me to soothe your wounded heart?"

"What would you know about feelings? Your heart is as cold and dead as the fish they barter in the market place."
"I have feelings, Anna. I just choose to expose them only when I feel the person is trustworthy enough to not abuse them."

"So you are saying you think I am abusive?"

"No! I am saying that I have only known you for a couple of days, and that is too short a time to determine your true motives towards me or anyone else."

"I have no time for playing games with people, Tyson. I cannot afford to lead others astray. What you see is what you get with me. If that is not enough for you, then move aside and let me pass."

He stretched himself to his full height and moved toward me. I had nowhere to go, but to stand my ground. He took the basket from my hands and placed it on the ground. He then took my hands in his, and pulled them to his lips, brushing a gentle kiss on each hand.

My pulse began to double, and the steely resolve I had mustered, crumbled like a crispy cookie. His eyes penetrated my soul once again, and I had no defense strong enough to resist.

"Who was the man in your dream, Anna?" The question sounded like a caress, and the tingling sensation started to course through my body again, but now it was as if it knew the path to take; it was no longer a stranger, but a welcome friend.

"Do you really have to ask, Tyson?" I said lowering my gaze. I felt defeated and I wanted him to be my champion and declare the very hope I clung to, that he felt the same way for me; that he loved me.

"Is it someone I know?"

"If it is not common knowledge to you by now, I am afraid my speaking it will not make it any more real."

I was pulled once again into his strong arms and he looked at me with such intensity, I felt my legs begin to quiver.

"I am a man of few words. I prefer action to dialogue." The kiss was fervent, with a need that seemed insatiable.

Panting, I regrettably pulled away from his hungry hold. "Was that supposed to be a declaration of some thing? I prefer words so that misunderstandings are avoided. Tyson, state your intentions towards me, or I shall leave this house today, and not look back."

"You are the only woman I have ever held in my arms. You are the only woman I have ever wanted to kiss. My heart is yours if you want it."

"You are in love with me, Tyson?"

"Yes, without a doubt. I love you, Anna."

Before I could reply, I heard the voice of Evirent invade my thoughts, and he seemed quite frantic to get my attention.

"Tyson, something is wrong. Evirent is looking for me. Something terrible is happening, and I have to find out what it is. Please forgive me, but I have to meet him right now in the clearing behind the barn."

I ran to the clearing, desperate to find out what could cause a dragon to be so agitated. Tyson ran with me, and not surprisingly, Joseph saw Evirent and called to Maria to come out right away. They followed closely behind.

Salvation

11

Evirent, saw us all rush into the clearing, and gave me a look of panic, if that is even possible for a dragon, but that is what it looked like, or maybe it was the feeling he was emitting to me in my mind.

"War is about to break out between the six Kingdoms, and you have the power to stop it."

"What is he talking about, Anna, how can you stop a war?" queried Tyson.

"Please do not interrupt with your questions. There is little time as it is. Your father has captured the five princes and is going to execute them today if you are not found. To retaliate against your father's actions, the other kingdoms have arrayed themselves into battle formation around the location, and they will slaughter everyone in your kingdom if he carries out this deed."

I can always count on my father to crush any happiness in my life. He is so good at evacuating the very essence from one's soul he should have been a vampire.

I turned to Tyson, Joseph and Maria, to explain what I knew I would eventually have to, but was hoping it did not have to be today. I longed to stay the plain young woman who had found her true love, and to live a simple life, burdened by tasks, and not by protocols and politics.

"My father is King Claude, and I am his daughter, Princess Annaliessa of Petroset."

The look of pure hatred that washed over Tyson's face in that instant froze me to my core.

"You are the daughter of the man who imprisoned and killed my mother?" snarled Tyson. "How did I not recognize you these past days? Do you possess the ability of magic as well that you have cast a spell on me, so as to torture me as your father did my mother?"

"Tyson, no, I did not cast any spell on you, and I would never dream of hurting you. I love you!"

"Just as my mother cursed your families, I too plan on further eradicating your family, and I will not stop until either I or your family is dead!"

The full force of what I had just heard was beginning to dawn on me, and I felt like I was dying inside. "I can understand your hatred of my father, but I am not like him, and your hatred will indeed lead to your destruction, Tyson," I pleaded.

How did I not associate the fact that he was a healer who knew some magic to the story he told, and that his mother would be the witch behind the curse?" He told me his mother died defending him. It all started to make sense, but I did not have the benefit of being able to process all the information at this moment. We both had kept secrets about who we were and they were about to crush us under their weight. *Was this why the woman in my dreams spoke to me? Was it Tyson's mother, and part of her revenge was to see me married to her son?"* If the plan was successful, it would indeed have ruined my father and tore apart the kingdom, and I had almost fallen victim to her scheme. This knowledge did absolutely nothing to ease the gut-wrenching pain radiating through my body. I also knew that my father had lied about executing Tyson's mother all those years ago, as she had only died last year. There was a great deal more to this story, and I was going to discover what it was one way or another.

"Evirent, take me to where my father intends to carry out this heinous act. I know what I need to do to stop it."

Once again, I found myself in the air and tried to choke back the sobs that wanted to rack my body. *How could he go from saying he loved me a few minutes earlier to hating me enough that he would want me dead? Why is it, the very man I finally fall in love with, is extricated from my embrace in a matter of moments? What cruel twist of fate is at play in my life? I am beginning to believe I am supposed to be miserable all my life. I was never meant to experience love and happiness, just duty and obligation.* Well at least I knew how duty and obligation performed, and I had become quite adept at it. I was going to find out just how much in a short amount of time.

Evirent flew in a pattern over the armies formed for battle, so as to gain the attention of every king. We needed a big entrance if a war was going to be thwarted, and lives were going to be spared. We needed them to hold back until I could address my father.

He began to descend into the square near the execution stand. The people screamed and ran to clear the space Evirent needed to land. The astonished look on the princes' faces was only surpassed by the look on my father's.

"Stop this nonsense right now, father! I am here, and there is no need for you to send us all to our death over such a foolish action."

My father never liked being commanded to do something by anyone, let alone a petulant woman like myself. The fury that emanated from him was more heated than any I had ever witnessed. "Where have you been sequestered these past couple of days, Annaliessa? Do you not care about the welfare of your family and these young men that are bound to you?" he growled.

"They are no longer bound to me, and I have a deal to broker that will satisfy their kingdoms and provide you what you desire as well."

"What do you mean they are no longer bound to you? What deal do you think you could offer that would be of value? How do I even know you remain unspoiled for your wedding night?"

"I have not compromised my wedding night in any way, and the fact that you would even question my integrity in such a way makes me nauseous. I broke the bond with the princes the night before the earthquake, by declaring my love for myself, and that I am not dependent on a man for such. The witch spoke to me that night, only I did not know it was her at the time, and she told me she released the bond."

"It is true, all of us felt the change that night, but we never had the opportunity to talk to Annaliessa about what happened," Jordan stated.

"Are you ready to hear my proposal to bring peace to our kingdoms?" I looked at each prince and then my father for affirmation.

"I think I speak for all of us princes, when I say we are willing to support a peaceful end to this dispute, and will immediately relay the proposal with our full support to our fathers," stated Jordan. All the other princes nodded in agreement.

"Annaliessa, you hold the rapt attention of us all," said my father snidely.

"The curse only applies to us royals if we marry others like ourselves. If we choose to marry someone who is not of this class, then the curse will be ineffective, and we will be able to bear as many children as we desire." The look of shock on everyone's face let me know I had their attention.

"I propose that over the next two years, on this date, when I have reached twenty and one years, if not sooner, I will choose whom I will marry, as will the princes. During the next two years, I will meet with every man, sixteen to twenty and five years, that has never been married or fathered a child, royal or not, if they so choose. I do not want to force anyone. The princes will do the same with all the virtuous young women."

I locked my gaze on each prince and asked them if they were willing to accept and participate in this plan. Each prince said they accepted it, but I saw the look of sorrow on Jordan's face. It seemed as if he was in agony with this decision, which perplexed me.

"Father, what say you?"

"I want this curse broken as much as the rest of you, but that is a very high price to pay to accomplish it. How do you know it will work?"

"The witch herself came to me in a dream and told me so. She intended for me to marry her son, but he was not so willing when he found out who my father was."

"Even in death that wretched woman torments me," King Claude whispered. "You met the witch's son? Is that who you have been with the past couple of days?" My father's hostility was palpable. He was shaking with it.

"He saved my life during the earthquake, but did not recognize who I was. I had no knowledge of him, so how could I have grasped who he was? While I did not plan for it, I think I am in love with him. So you will do nothing to him, as you owe him my life. Besides, I do not think he intends to harm me in any way, as he loves me, or at least he did up until the moment he found out who I really was. Do we have an understanding on this matter, father?"

My father seemed to mull this over. I knew he was calculating how this would benefit him. I knew all too well he would not give up the power and control he had mustered so easily. I was still concerned for Tyson's safety, regardless of my father's reply. He was not known for his honesty.

"It shall be as you say. Release the princes so they can bring the terms to their kingdoms."

All the princes bore the look of shock at my declaration about Tyson. Jordan, however, looked as if someone had just run him through with a sword and he struggled to maintain his footing. The look of horrific pain etched his features, and I watched as two tears made their downward course on his cheeks. Something with steel sharp teeth was gnawing on my heart strings, and I could not hold his gaze; it was sucking the air out of my lungs.

The princes were to ride Evirent back to their armies to bring the news of the settlement. I saw Jordan hesitate to ride off to his father's army. He seemed conflicted, but he had an obligation to fulfill, and that had to come before anything else. I was sure we would talk soon, as I was anxious to hear from the princes how they knew the bond had been broken, what it really felt like, and if they were happy about it. I nodded to Jordan to acknowledge what he could not say, and then turned my attention back to my father.

"Father, I intend to start with the young men in the prison first thing in the morning."

"I forbid you to seek prisoners as a potential husband. How are you going to marry a man that is set for execution? How are you to have a wedding night with someone in a cell?"

"I will focus on the ones not sentenced to death as of today, and have the opportunity of freedom in the next two years, based on their crime and the prescribed punishments set into law today. You will not have the opportunity to change sentencing or set executions because you find it detestable to think I could choose such a man. You gave your word in front of the entire village, and you know you can not retract your agreement."

"By the way, there was a very kind family that gave me shelter the past couple of days, and I want them rewarded. I would like to personally deliver their gifts in the next day or so. I will send word to you of what I wish to bestow on them."

"Is this where the witch's son is staying as well?" my father asked, but it came out more like a demand.

"I have no idea where he is staying at this moment. He was very angry about me being your daughter, and he certainly is holding a lot of hostility toward whatever you did to his mother."

"His mother deserved what she received."

"Why not tell me the story and let me decide for myself if that is true, or if he has a genuine right to be so enraged at the lack of justice?"

"I do not have to explain anything to you, Annaliessa. I am done speaking with you. Go see your mother."

"Where is my mother?"

A maid stepped forward from the crowd and said that she would take me to her. I left my father seething in the square, and could not be more pleased. Normally, I would be overjoyed at the prospect of what tomorrow would bring, but my heart was still raw from the betrayal of Tyson. I had no idea if two years would be long enough to recover from the devastation of that loss, let alone give me time to fall in love again.

The Cost of Bread

12

I will admit I was nervous about going to the prison. This was only the temporary one, being that the one in the castle was no longer available, and should not prove to be as frightening, but it was a place I had never been, so I had no idea what to expect.

I had a full contingent of knights guarding me, and it was intimidating to say the least. The boy they introduced me to was a little taken aback by it. Who could blame him?

"What is your name, and what is the crime you are charged with?" I asked. He was average height, with brown hair and unusual green eyes. He was quite wide and thick, but not in an obese way. He had a body that suggested he was made to labor in the fields, where heavy lifting would be required.

"My name is Brandon, Princess. I was caught stealing bread and fruit in the market for my eight siblings."

"Brandon, why is it that you are responsible for feeding your siblings?"

"My father was killed working in the king's mines several moon cycles ago. My mother died giving birth to my youngest brother, two years ago. Given that there was no one else to take care of my siblings when I went to prison a fortnight and a half past, they have been spread out to family members, as no one could care for all of them together."

"Do you not yet have a trade that will earn you a living?"

"I am the oldest in my family, at nineteen years, and I had the responsibility of looking after the house while my father worked. I had a brother just over a year younger than me, but he died as a child. My oldest sister turned fifteen years last sun's zenith and my father had her married off days later. She is expecting her first child, and she is looking after my youngest brother right now. I have three sisters after her, who are thirteen, twelve and ten years. My father would have married off my sister when she turned fourteen, but perhaps now she will have an opportunity to wait at least another year. I think my aunt may want her around to help raise her twin girls, who are now just four years. She has five boys, and having a girl around the house seems to have her in good spirits for now. I have an uncle who took my three remaining brothers who are eleven, eight and six years, as his wife has been unable to have children. An aunt on my father's side took in my other two sisters, and has put them to work to help earn their keep by sewing and doing laundry. Hard tasks for girls so young, do you not agree?"

"Yes, it sounds like life has been hard in general for you and your family. Brandon, if I can manage to provide a way for you to be set free so that you can apprentice and learn a trade to pay off your debt, would you be interested?"

"I would do anything to get out of here and help my siblings, Your Highness."

"Give me a couple of days to make arrangements and ascertain the terms of your release. Once I have word, I will come and see you again."

"You are not anything like what I expected."

"Is that good or bad?"

56

"Definitely good. You are not like any royal I have ever met. It is unfortunate Tyson cannot see that."

I was surprised the news of Tyson had reached even the prison. *Was my pain to be on public display and open for taunting?*

"You know Tyson?"

"Yes, he helped me once when I was sick as a boy of thirteen years. His herbs drew the sickness out of my body. After that, we became friends."

"Brandon, do you know what happened to him and his mother to cause him to hate my father, and now me, so viciously?"

"Yes, but I will not share that with you today. When you come back and I am free, I will gladly tell you the tale."

"Very well, you can keep your secret until we meet again. Thank-you, Brandon, I have enjoyed our time very much."

The knights wasted no time in sweeping me up and out of the prison. They looked relieved to have me outside and on my way back to my new, temporary dwelling.

It would take a couple of years, but my father already had trees being felled where the new castle would be erected. It is a good thing he had so many slaves (or what they really are, prisoners), to do his laborious work. I had a new appreciation for their plight. I wondered how many others were lying in this prison for doing what comes naturally; providing for starving family members.

Release and Prosperity

13

All night I thought about how I could not only make things better for Brandon, but for others like him. Without a trade, he would end up a beggar for life, and given how unrelenting my father was in the way of forgiveness of trespasses, his life would be short.

Normally, and if they were fortunate, fathers trained their children in the trade they had learned from their father or a family member. Orphans should have the same opportunity, especially ones with younger siblings they are responsible for.

I had sent word to my father that I urgently needed to speak to him about a kingdom matter first thing in the morning, and was lucky to have been granted the audience with him. Now all I had to do was get my father to agree to it. If he saw how it benefited him, I knew he would put his stamp of approval on it.

I dragged myself out of bed the next morning full of expectation of a new future for Brandon and others like him. Perhaps the other kingdoms would even put this into action, but then I was getting ahead of myself. If it was not for the promise I had made to Brandon to try to get him released, I would not have left my bed. My head ached only slightly less than my heart, and my body felt heavy, like a water-soaked blanket. I went through the motions of dressing and morning routines in a dream-like state, not really sure how it all had managed to happen as I stared at my presentable form. *Will this pain-filled fog ever lift, or is this what I can expect to welcome me to each day?* I wondered, not really expecting an answer.

I made my way to the throne room and waited to be recognized by the King. In this room, he was not my father, but my King, and I would have to remember my place if I wanted a successful outcome.

"Annaliessa, you may come forward and state your business," my father proclaimed. "Does this have something to do with the request for gifts for the couple that housed you? If it is, I will save you some time; I have agreed to the list, and have sent instructions to my treasurer to give you what you have asked for. You may deliver it when you are ready, but you must take a contingent of knights along with you, and you must let me know when you are leaving and when you are expected to return."

I was nervous, which was unusual for me. "Thank-you, but it is another matter I want to address. I have come to see that we have a number of orphans in our kingdom that, if given the right opportunity, could become taxpayers for the King."

"Go on, I am listening."

"Normally, village children are taught the trade of their fathers. However, when these men die and leave a wife with many mouths to feed, or in some cases, where there is no longer even a mother, these children end up as beggars, or worse, thieves in your prison for taking the very necessities of life. Your Excellency I implore you to establish an apprenticeship program for these people. They can be trained as farmers, carpenters, mason workers, blacksmiths, or even bakers. As part of their wages, they would receive food from the kingdom's resources so they can feed their families while learning a skill, at a reduced wage to entice the master trades to take on additional apprentices. Once they have successfully learned this skill, they will then have a trade they can employ and earn the money they need to provide the necessities and go from beggars, or wards of the kingdom's resources, to taxpayers, allowing others to follow the same course. Given our need for trades-people to rebuild our home, this seems like a prudent course of action, does it not?"

I held my breath in anticipation of his reply. I never thought silence could be so loud, but I found it assaulting my senses in a most acute manner as I tried to remain still.

"I agree we need the trades people, and slaves only take from the resources, while providing the work necessary. Your proposal has merit, and I agree to try it for the next two years. Whether it continues after that will depend on how many new taxpayers actually result."

"Your Excellency, may I make one more proposal for you to consider this day?"

"As long as it will be quick, I have other matters to attend to."

"There is an orphaned young man in the prison right now who is there due to a situation as I have presented in my previous proposal. I would like to ask if he could be the first to take advantage of this generous provision you have made possible."

"Is he likely to become my son-in-law?" my Father said sarcastically.

"I have no interest in him beyond making it possible for him to aid his younger siblings."

"If you find a suitable apprenticeship for him, he will be released, but he must pay back the value of what he stole from his earnings. He will not receive a single gran of those wages until what he owes has been satisfied. Is this understood?"

"Of course, Your Excellency. I will see to his apprenticeship myself."

I bowed and left the throne room, excited to put my plan into motion. I hope Brandon could appreciate how distasteful it was for me to grovel at my father's feet, but sometimes, we all have to eat a little humble pie for the greater good. While my father was not going to afford him even the smallest of our monetary value, a single gran, until his debt was repaid, I was not going to see him released from prison empty handed. I also knew just the blacksmith I would ask to apprentice Brandon, as his oldest son had married and gone on to work in the king's armory, and his other children were all girls.

I was quite pleased with myself by the end of the day. I had an apprenticeship in place for Brandon, and he would be released tomorrow. His home had been claimed by his debt to the baker and the fruit merchant, and he would not be allowed to return to it until the debt was paid. I decided I would find him lodging at Joseph and Maria's. It would give me an opportunity to see if Tyson was still there, and perhaps try to reason with him. I had come to the conclusion that we were never going to be together, but I could not bear the thought of him hating me forever.

Injustice Clarified

14

I met Brandon outside of the prison. The smile on his face was enormous, and it looked like he wanted to embrace me in a bone crunching hug, but caught himself when the knights beside me took a step in front of me. They had also read his intentions.

He bowed and said, "May I take the liberty of addressing the Princess?"

"You may," I stated, with a smile tugging at the corners of my mouth. How different our exchange was today, than it was a couple of days ago. I always hated this formality. I would have preferred the hug. At least it was an honest display of gratitude. This was so contrived and awkward.

"I wish to express my deepest appreciation for the kindness you have bestowed on me. I can never repay you or truly express how much this means to me, to have my freedom, and a way to help my family."

"Brandon, you are most welcome. I hope that your freedom and new found employment will bring you great blessings, and perhaps even a wife."

"Do you know someone who would be interested in that occupation, your highness?"

"Not to my knowledge, but I am sure you will have many admirers in short order."

"I think they want me to ride in my carriage, but I want to travel along side you, so that you can tell me the story you promised. Since there is no way they will allow you to ride in the carriage, we can ride in the open wagon that carries some of the gifts for Joseph and Maria, the couple who will house you for the time being."

The captain of the knights gave me a stern look and started to open his mouth to protest this idea, but I held up my hand and said, "I will be in plain sight so you can be sure nothing inappropriate is happening between us. If I choose to not ride in comfort, what is that to you? I have no intentions of complaining, so I see no further need for discussion."

Having said that, I looked at Brandon and nodded my head for him to follow me to the wagon.

"Now that we have begun our journey, Brandon, I beg you to tell me the story about Tyson and his mother."

"Princess, I am not sure it is my story to tell, but I did say that I would share it if you were able to set me free, and so I see no way to back down from my word."

"You did not think that I would be able to garner your freedom, did you?"

"I am afraid you have exposed me for the skeptic I am," he said with a blush forming on his face.

"I have to tell you that the story is quite gruesome, and I am not sure if your delicate constitution can handle the sordid details, Princess."

"Do not be concerned, I assure you, I am not as delicate as I appear."

"It all started when Tyson was five and in school. He struggled with reading more than most."

"I am sorry to interrupt, but I do know about this part. What I want to know is what did the teacher do to him, and how it ended up with his mother in prison for seventeen years?"

"The man used Tyson as a man would use a woman, and had sexual relations with him."

I sucked in my breath and held it for a moment before exhaling it in a stuttered gasp. Tears began to sting my eyes, but I could not let them overtake me, or he may not continue.

"Are you alright, Princess?"

"Yes, please continue, Brandon."

"His mother, Leah, went to the King, your father, and asked for him to punish the teacher for this insane cruelty to her son. She wanted him to be put to death; which he should have been, under the law. Your father never liked Leah, and so he refused to even put him in prison. When the other parents found out about what was happening, they became concerned for their children and they all went to the King demanding that he be punished. Your father could not deny this many of his subjects, but he still refused to execute him, and instead only put him in prison."

"Is this why Leah placed the curse on our families; because of my father's insensitivity to Tyson's plight?"

"Yes. She wanted your father to understand what it was like to be powerless over his child and your destiny. That is the reason for the curse of only being able to be with child once, and then being bonded to the other kingdoms' offspring as well."

"Your father knew it would be difficult to execute her, let alone hold her in prison, given her power. Besides, she warned him that if he killed her, she would be able to visit him even in her death, and that her vengeance would seek its reward, even after she was gone. Your father had a special cell made for her in the dungeon.

He had a dragon slain, and painted the walls with its blood. The dragon's blood contains powerful magic, a magic even older than Leah's own. To be extra cautious, he even had a warlock enchant the cell as well."

"I can see why the dragons hate my father. His wickedness knows no bounds."

"The worst part of her imprisonment was that her cell was next to the man who had molested Tyson."

"What? How horribly cruel!" I shouted. My outrage was beginning to reach the boiling point, and I was barely able to contain it.

"I wish the ghastliness of it ended there. Tyson was allowed to visit his mother regularly. Every time he would come face to face with his tormentor. His love for his mother gave him the courage to return, but the nightmares were horrendous afterwards. The dragon's blood in the cell not only kept his mother captive and made her powers ineffective, but it gradually drained her of her life. Tyson had to watch her die bit by bit while being taunted by the man who ripped away his very innocence and held him hostage to the ordeal every night in his dreams."

I could not hold back the tears, and they flowed like a river during the thaw of the snow. My body shook with the anguish of a boy and a mother denied justice, persecuted, and then abandoned by a king who was to be their protector. It is no longer a mystery as to why Tyson could go from love to hate in an instant. I represented everything corrupt and evil in his life, and there was no way I could undo the damage that had been stamped onto his soul with a branding iron.

The depravity my father conveyed was astounding. It is the kind that burrows deep roots into one's innermost being. He was indeed rotten to the core, and I would have to find a way to articulate his sins so that he would be ashamed and stripped of any dignity whatsoever. He did not deserve to carry the title King, or even human being for that matter. I turned and leaned over the side of the wagon and regurgitated. *Well so much for proving I am not 'delicate',* I thought to myself.

Charity's Reward

15

We had arrived at Joseph and Maria's, and the door opened with an astonished Maria seeing the caravan of gifts, and me being helped out of the back of the wagon.

She ran towards me with her arms outstretched, only to be denied the physical contact she invited by the knights. I rolled my eyes, and let out an agitated breath. "Leave her alone, she means me no harm. Allow her to pass."

The knights took a small step to the side and Maria launched herself through the gap, almost knocking me to my backside with the force of her hug. I laughed, and hugged her fiercely back. It was not often I had the comforts of human affection, and I was starving for it.

She finally pulled back with tears in her eyes, and said, "I was not sure I would ever see you again, Princess Annaliessa. I was so worried for your well-being when you flew off on that dragon. I heard of the heroic thing you did in saving the princes. It was all any of the villagers could talk about, well until what you did for the orphans. Do you have any idea the respect and loyalty the people have bestowed upon you?"

"I hardly think doing the right thing deserves any special mention or consideration. I am only trying to right some of the wrongs that have been perpetrated over the past couple of decades. I hope the people have not put me in such a place of honor that the only way for me to proceed is down. Please, share my dismay at their adoration. I am not worthy."

"Princess Annaliessa, the very fact that you would say you are not worthy, means you are. For a young woman of nobility, you are exceptionally humble, and it makes you all the more appealing."

I blushed deeply, and felt such an overwhelming sense of gratitude at that moment that I was incapable of forming words. I noticed that tears had started trickling down my face, and I had to turn to wipe them away before I made a complete fool of myself. I really needed a distraction, and Brandon took the cue.

"My name is Brandon, Madam Maria. I am most grateful that you have allowed me the opportunity to room in your home."

Maria gazed at Brandon with a maternal smile and acceptance. "Brandon, any friend of the princess, is a friend of ours. We were so pleased with the request; we have all been aflutter with excitement for your arrival. Even Tyson seems to have cheered up a bit knowing you were coming to stay with us."

At the mention of his name, my stomach twisted in a knot, and my heartbeat sped up. I wanted to see him again so badly, even if the only emotion that he would return would be hate. I did not care. I would have to live off of that for now, as it was better than living in the fog of desperation.

"Is he here now, Maria?" She must have seen the plea in my eyes that ached with anticipation for an affirmative answer.

She leaned in close to my ear and said, "He is not. He does want to address you at some point before you go, and he said you would know where to find him, and that you should come alone. He promised he would not harm you."

Joseph came from around the back of the house just then, and I saw him break into a gregarious grin. "Welcome back Princess Annaliessa. You have been missed."

"Thank-you, Joseph, you and Maria are so kind and generous with your welcome. Joseph, I would like to introduce you to Brandon."

The two men formally introduced themselves and sized each other up. While they did this familiar ritual, I gave my command to the knights. "Joseph will instruct you on where everything should be stored, please do as he asks. I am going to go in to say hello to Tabitha, their baby girl. I do not need an escort, as I am sure the worst a baby can do is soil my clothing."

I linked my arm with Maria's and we headed to the house. Once inside, I took a quick peek at Tabitha, kissing her on her forehead as she slept. "Maria, I have to head to the woods to find Tyson. I do not have a great deal of time, as I must be back fast enough for the knights to not notice that I have disappeared."

"Go. I will stall them if you are not back on time."

I ran out the back and into the woods to find the willow tree where Tyson had taken my heart. The memory of his passionate kiss left me feeling lightheaded and warm. I had no expectation of reclaiming my heart as it was his to keep unless he returned it. I prayed silently that he would be amenable to mending our relationship in some degree at least.

Lover's Quarrel

16

I practically ran the entire way to the tree. My legs were fuelled with hope and propelled me to my destination as if I was being pulled by some mysterious force.

I arrived and called out to Tyson. The hanging branches parted and he stepped onto the path. I lost all sense of reason at the sight of his handsome face. It was a face I was made to caress and kiss. A face with lips that were meant to set me ablaze with pleasure, and eyes that were meant to capture and detain me in their loving stare.

I hesitantly stammered out, "You, w-w-wanted to see m-me?"

"I understand I was quite rude with you a few days ago. I apologize for my behavior, but I was taken off guard with what I had learned so abruptly. I have spent fourteen years hating your father, and at that moment I could not separate the hate for him from you. I know you are not the evil person your father is, and I wish to have the opportunity you have extended to every young man of the kingdom; to be considered for marriage to the princess. You obviously still love me, or you would never have come out here alone."

"You want to be considered for marriage? A few days ago you wanted me dead, and now am I honestly to believe that you want to marry me?" I could not explain it, but something did not ring true about what he said. I heard the echo of his mother's voice from the dream, and her encouragement of marriage. As much as I wanted what he said to be true, I knew deep down it was not, and it was strangling me, making it hard to breathe normally. I had to really concentrate to stay relaxed, and not let on that I knew he was lying. *How could I have been so blind to this truth before? Perhaps witchcraft was involved and I was under its spell until today.*

"I never wanted you dead, just your family. Killing you would be a travesty, especially when you have captured the heart of the people you will some day reign over."

"Tyson, surely you must know that my father will never condone such a request. I will never be allowed to marry you. My father would kill me himself if I even so much as suggest it. Is that what you were hoping, that he would do the dirty deed for you so that you would not look like the bad guy?"

"Honestly, Annaliessa, do you really think I am that hard-hearted?"

"I cannot honestly say anything about you right now. Everything I had believed was based on a lie, and all I have left to cling to is the hope that somewhere the little boy who was so brutally abandoned wants to be loved after all. I love that part of you Tyson, the part that deserves to be loved and accepted, and to be restored to wholeness. I want that so desperately for you. I want to be the one to offer it to you, but the chasm that has separated us by hate, is too wide to cross, I am afraid."

"You speak of love and restoration, but the only thing I really hear you saying is that I am not worthy of receiving it. You talk a good game, Annaliessa, but that is all it is, talk. You know nothing about healing a broken heart, especially that of a man. Your only focus is on yourself, and I find it rather distasteful."

"The last thing in this world that I am focused on is my desires and comforts, you bastard! How dare you!"

"Oh, so you have heard the story then?"

"What story are you referring to Tyson? The one about your childhood, or the one about the time your mother spent in prison?"

"Neither actually, rather it is the story of my conception. You see, I really am a bastard. My mother was raped by one of the king's knights. My mother did not get any justice then either. Your father laughed it off as 'men behaving like men', and taking what they need. The only consolation my mother had was me. She loved me in spite of how I came about. My father met an untimely death, however. Quite a painful one from the way mother told me it. Hence the reason your father was frightened of my mother, and why he disliked her so much."

"I am sorry. I did not know. I am not my father, Tyson. I am not your foe. I want to help you, but you have left me no other choice as long as you harbor such hatred in your heart. I was hoping we could at least be friends, but how is that possible when every time you look at me, all you see is my father? I should not have come to see you, and I beg your forgiveness if I have injured you further in any way. It was not intentional, I assure you."

"You may be beautiful to behold, Annaliessa, but your heritage is dark and ugly. It will be your ruin, and I will hold the key to the carnage that is unleashed. I see now my attempt at winning your heart was foolish."

"You are a blind fool, Tyson! You already have my heart. You have control over what happens to it. I gave you that power when you kissed me under this very tree."

"Truth be told, I have no need of your heart, Princess, at this point, just your bed will suffice."

I inhaled sharply, and glared at Tyson with an icy stare. "Well I guess there is one thing you will no longer have and one thing you will never have; my heart and my bed."

The laugh that came from his throat chilled me to the bone. I was truly frightened. I did not want to give him the satisfaction of having me cower, but I could not stomach the wave of evil that was emanating off of him. I had no choice but to turn and run, I needed to put as much distance between me and Tyson as I possibly could, and I needed to do it fast.

What an idiot I was to think I could somehow change him. You cannot change a man's character by sheer will, or even with love, if he is unwilling to receive that love or wants to remain as he is.

Tyson was hell bent on destruction, and I was just a pawn to be played in the game of revenge, nothing more.

I had been childish in my thinking and in my desires, and was finding the learning curve into adulthood was steeper than I had prepared for.

Invitation

17

I was still reeling from the exchange I had with Tyson two days ago. I feared I had responded as a novice young girl in the realm of adult love. I now believe I was just caught up in the physical aspect of his kiss. I had no idea, really. I had only ever been kissed once before, and now that I dwell on that experience, I remember feeling something similar to what I experienced with Tyson, only not as intense. *Was that because of the whole curse, and not really being alone like I was with Tyson? Was part of the intrigue of his kiss the fact that we were secluded without fear of being caught, so we could let our physical responses wander without abandon? Why did I have so many questions? I am driving myself insane with them. Can I even trust myself to know love when it crosses my path?* I wanted to ask my mother these questions, but she has never known the experience of love, so she would not be able to aid in my quest for revelation on this matter. I only knew one woman for certain who could answer my questions, and receiving a warm invitation to visit the kingdom of Vulterrian, was unlikely. In fact, receiving a warm welcome or invitation to any of the kingdoms was unlikely after the thwarted execution attempt of the princes. I certainly could not expect any of them to come to me. Their parents would never allow them to be anywhere close to my father again which, in turn, meant nowhere near me as well. They had their freedom from the bond and the marriage to me, so I was nothing more than collateral damage, even though I did save their lives.

I heard a knock at my bedroom door and got up from my musings to find out who would be interested in my attention.

"Your Highness, an invitation has just arrived from the Vulterrian Kingdom."

I saw the messenger from Jordan's kingdom standing at the ready to relay the message. "Go ahead, speak your message."

"The Prince of Vulterrian requests the presence of the Princess of Petroset at a royal ball. You are invited to stay as long as you wish. You will need to leave today in order to arrive on time for the event."

"I would be most honored to fulfill the prince's request by attending the royal ball and spending time in his kingdom. I will send word to my mother, and will prepare to leave within two hours, assuming a suitable escort can be gathered for my trip."

"I will be most delighted to escort you to Vulterrian, Your Highness."

Just the invitation I was hoping for! Now maybe I could get some answers, assuming Queen Sarah would give me an audience. I was excited at the prospect and that was not something I had felt for far too long.

Secret Proposal

18

I had only been shown to my room at the Vulterrian castle when I heard a knock behind one of the wall panels.

I moved toward the sound of the knocking, and tapped the wall. "Annaliessa, it is Jordan. Are you alone? May I come in? I really need to talk to you."

"Yes, I am alone. How do I let you in?"

The wall panel slid open, and Jordan stood at the threshold, uncertain if he should cross. I yanked him over it quickly and asked him how to close it. He showed me the hidden latch, and showed me how to use it.

"So, you have a secret passage way to my room. Do all the rooms connect to yours, or just mine?"

"Your room was hand picked by me, rest assured. I wanted to be able to talk to you without anyone prying. So I hope you will forgive the simple nature of the room. It is not one of the grand guest rooms, but rather a room we would normally use for guests with less importance. I will show you the way through the passage so you can find my room and a special place I want to show you."

"Annaliessa, I hope you will forgive my lack of proper decorum and protocol, but ever since that night I sensed the bond had been broken, I have so desperately wanted to speak with you."

"Jordan, you know there are no apologies needed where we are concerned. Please speak whatever is on your mind. I am not sure I have all the answers you are seeking, but I will tell you whatever I know."

"Do you still love him?"

"You certainly do not waste time going straight for the tough questions do you?"

"I have to know the answer to that question before any of the others will matter."

"I am not sure what I feel right now, Jordan. I am very confused. There is no doubt that he does not love me. He made that perfectly clear. He had the audacity to ask me to consider him for marriage, which was only a ploy for his real desire, revenge."

"So you have seen him recently then?" Concern was etched in his voice.

"I saw him when I delivered the gifts to the couple that housed me after the earthquake. He wanted me to think he cared for me, but the truth was something quite different."

"Did he kiss you when you were with him, after the earthquake, I mean?"

"Jordan, why does any of this matter?" I said frustrated. I was really hoping for a way out of answering him.

"Did it feel differently to kiss someone after the bond had been broken, than what it felt like when I kissed you?"

"Are you asking me because you are curious for yourself and what you can expect, or is there another reason for your question?"

I was very uncomfortable with this line of questioning from Jordan. *I hope I am not showing just how disturbed I am. Please let him only be curious for himself. I am not sure I can handle the other option.*

"I have only ever kissed one person, and that was you while under the bond. I want to know what it is like now that it is no longer a factor."

His voice was not the steady rhythm I was accustomed to, so I really need to be careful how I respond to this, as I do not want to hurt his feelings or his pride. "I do not think that I am the best judge on the issue, Jordan. I have only known heartbreak as a result of it, and I would not wish that on you or any of the other princes."

"Does he still claim your heart, Annaliessa?" he asked tenderly, but I could see the alarm hiding behind his eyes.

"Jordan, I am not sure if I claim my heart right now. I really was hoping to have an opportunity to speak with your mother about this topic, since she knows the way of love with a man."

"I will arrange time for you to speak to her before dinner then," he said with a bit more cheeriness to his voice.

"Thank-you, you always make me feel better. You have done that since we were kids."

"Annaliessa, do you remember the time during the sun's zenith you spent here when you were nine years?"

"Yes, it is one of my fondest memories, actually. I always enjoyed being away from home, but never so much as when I was here."

"Do you remember how I taught you to climb the tree in the garden?"

"I remember the scandal that expedition caused. You would have thought we had been caught stealing gold out of the treasury the way everyone carried on about it."

"Do you know what I remember?"

"What is it that you remember, Jordan?"

"The way your hair smelled like lavender and jasmine. The way you fit so nicely against me as you leaned your back to my chest. The euphoric happiness of that day fills my memory every time I think of you, when I hear your name, or when I look upon your precious face. How we were both so happy that we fell asleep like that, together in the tree, completely content."

"Jordan," I let out a sigh. "It is funny you should mention that story. My mother reminded me of it not long ago. She also told me an interesting piece about that time that I did not know. Do you have any idea what she told me?"

"I am guessing it would be how I told everyone that I was going to marry you after that day."

"Yes, that was what she said. So you are verifying its accuracy?"

"Annaliessa, I have never hidden my feelings for you from anyone, except maybe the one person I should have been bolder with, and that person is you."

"I have loved you since before the bond started, and I have no desire to stand back now and have you married to another man. Annaliessa, I want to be considered for your hand in marriage."

"Jordan, you know what that means!" I protested. "You and I can only be with child once. Is that really what you want? It most certainly is not what is best for your kingdom."

"I want to show you the way through the secret passage to my room and the special place I want to share with you tonight after dinner and the festivities have ended. Tonight I will share with you why this proposal is not as crazy as it seems. Will you agree to come and meet me and hear what I have to say?"

"Jordan, when have I ever said no to you?"

"If I asked you to marry me right now, does that mean you will say yes?"

"You are such an incorrigible pest!" I said laughing. "Show me this secret passage and the place you want to meet me at tonight."

With that I was off on another adventure with Jordan. He was always such fun to be with. I had forgotten this detail of our relationship, as things had gotten so much more formal as we had left our childhood years and the bonding had set in. It was almost as if I was nine years young again, and he was showing me some form of mischievous game he had invented. For the first time in days, my heart did not feel so heavy, and I was anxious to hear what he wanted to share tonight.

Love's Counsel

19

Jordan had shown me to a sheltered tower that had a gorgeous view of the ocean. If I lived here, I would spend a great deal of time in this very spot. I could see why he loved this place most of all. The sound of the waves caressing the shore was so peaceful and majestic. It made me understand how insignificant I really am in the grandness of nature.

I could not coax him into telling me his proposal early. He wanted to tell me tonight, and no amount of prying was going to make him unseal his lips and part with the secret. I had to respect him. He was true to his word, and was every bit the gentleman while we were alone. *Was I hoping he would not be somehow? I really was messed up. I hope Queen Sarah can help unravel the tangle of thoughts that are knotted up in my head.* I was no longer sure I could trust myself with anything, and Jordan did not need me to unload this chaotic whirlwind on him.

I returned to my room and unpacked my things. I was feeling a sense of accomplishment when a knock came at my door.

"Princess Annaliessa, I am here to escort you to the Queen. She has time to speak with you and has requested your company."

"Please, take me to her then."

Queen Sarah was a blond, brown-eyed beauty, and was enjoying a reclining pose at a window looking toward the river to the south. "Welcome Annaliessa, please have a seat and get comfortable, my dear."

"Thank-you very much for your kindness, Queen Sarah."

"Annaliessa, we can dispense with the formalities while we are here in this place together. My son tells me you wanted to speak with me about how you are feeling. Is it about loving a man?"

"It probably seems odd that I would want to ask you these questions and not my own mother. It is just that you and King Nicholas are the only two people I know of the royal families that seem to honestly love each other. So you seemed like the best person to ask."

"I do not find it odd. What you said is true. All the other couples were married out of obligation, and not for love. It is the one thing I have always admired about you, Annaliessa. You have always stated, since you were a little girl, that you were going to marry a prince who loved you, not one that you had to marry."

"However, now, I imagine since the eligible bachelors have increased thousands of times from the original five, it seems rather daunting to know if love is even possible in so short a time."

"Yes, it is one of the things that create some distress for me, but it is not the real source of my confusion. I am not sure what love is supposed to feel or be like. How do you know when you are truly in love with someone, or if it is just some infatuation due to lack of experience in such matters?"

"Would this confusion have to do with Tyson, the witch's son?"

"Yes, he is a factor, but if I am being honest, so is your son. We have been friends ever since we were little children, and I am not sure where the line of friendship ends and love that brings two people to marry begins."

"How did you feel when you were with Tyson?"

"I am embarrassed to have to say, Your Majesty. He made me feel like I was on fire and I wanted to be with him in reckless abandon which is anything but proper. I had never wanted someone like that before, and it was intoxicating."

"How do you feel when you are with Jordan?"

"I feel safe and happy. He always knows what to say to make me laugh. He is full of adventure, and he is fun to be with as a result. He will make a great king one day, I am sure of that."

"Which of those two feelings do you think will last longer?"

"Well, based on my limited experience, not the first one. That ended the moment he discovered I was supposed to be his mortal enemy."

"That feeling, Annaliessa, is common to everyone. Everyone desires something forbidden, or inaccessible. It is intoxicating, as you stated. The problem is it does not last. It comes and goes, just as the seasons have their appointed times, so does this feeling. It can be quite overpowering in the moment, and has caused many to stray and end up in all kinds of compromising situations."

"Love is more than a feeling, or an emotion, Annaliessa. It is a commitment to another that transcends yourself. It is a choice to share ones self, without reservation, with another. It is based on trust and loyalty. Without these, it cannot exist. It is born out of friendship and the sincere desire to want the other person in your life forever. Love is deeper than the feeling that ebbs like the oceans tides. It is more like the rock that is immovable. It never falters, and it remains true under all kinds of distress, and it withstands the tests of time. Ask yourself if you would miss this person if they were never around, and what it would be like for you if you never saw them again. Is it just a feeling you are missing, or is there something deeper that causes the sense of loss? Now tell me, is this what you had with Tyson?"

"No, it most certainly was not."

"My son feels this way about you, Annaliessa. He always has, and I am afraid he always will. We had always thought the two of you would make a great couple. He has never talked about marrying anyone but you. Annaliessa, if you cannot have what I just described to you for my son, then I implore you to not lead him to believe otherwise. It will hurt him deeply for you to reject him, but it is better you do it now, so he still has time to find love with another."

"Queen Sarah, the last thing I ever want to do is hurt Jordan. I also would never do him the disservice of leading him to believe I have feelings I do not have. The truth is I am not entirely sure what my feelings are and if I truly believe what you described is what Jordan and I can have with each other. I need more time to figure it out, and I am grateful for your invitation to allow me some time to explore this possibility. I am surprised anyone would be willing to entertain me in any way, given my father's actions. I hold no ill will toward the other kingdoms for it, but am grateful you have indulged me this kindness."

"You are not your father, Annaliessa, and I would never judge you for his sins."

"You have no idea how much what you just said means to me. It is not surprising that Jordan bears your forgiving and kind spirit."

"I look forward to seeing you tonight at dinner. If you need to speak with me again, please have one of the servants get message to me."

"Thank-you, Your Majesty," I said as I bowed and left the room.

I had a better understanding of where I stood on love. I was idiotic and naïve to believe I was in love with Tyson; that was just my feelings going into irrational and foreign places I had not known before. I was not sure if I could call what Jordan and I had love, or just friendship. *We were definitely friends, but were we more than that? Well, I was more than that for him, but was it reciprocated by me?*

Jealousy's Arrival

20

Time stands still when you are anticipating something special. The expectation of Jordan's secret had bored itself deep in my brain and I was slowly going mad with anticipation. The afternoon seemed terminal, and I did not have the cure.

It was late afternoon, about the time one normally readies oneself for the evening meal. A maid was sent to my bedroom to prepare me for dinner. I had made my dress selection about two hours ago, after trying on each of the fifteen dresses I had brought with me at least twice. I wanted to look stunning, and for the first time in my life, I really cared about what I looked like. *Was this part of being in love, or was I trying to manufacture feelings that were not there?*

I was shocked to see the maid carrying an amazing sky blue dress with intricate beadwork on the bodice and handmade golden lace ribbons that cascaded from the waist band all the way to the floor. "That is not my dress. You must have the wrong room," I said to the maid.

"No, Your Highness, I was specifically told that you were to wear this to dinner and the ball this evening."

"Who told you I was to wear it?"

"His Highness, the Prince, of course. He told me he would be very displeased if you arrived for dinner in anything else."

"I would not want you to be in any kind of trouble for disobeying his instructions, so I will oblige you, and wear the dress." I said this so it came across casually, as if I was a bit reluctant, but inside, my heart skipped a beat.

I spent the next hour having my makeup and hair done. The dress was spectacular, and made my eyes stand out even more than usual. I had never felt so beautiful in all my life. I had been told I was pretty in the past, but for the first time I actually saw it, and I felt a bit self-conscious. The sad part was, at the end of the night, the dress would come off and the beautiful woman staring in the gleaming polished metal reflecting frame would be no more. I would be the simple, pretty princess I had always been. Nothing remarkable to look at, but not unpleasant either. At least with this dress and the way my hair and makeup looked tonight, I would have a better chance of standing out from the truly beautiful girls of the kingdom, who would be vying for Jordan's attention.

The sound of the bells ringing in the hallway told me it was time to descend to the dining room. I took a deep breath to calm myself, and opened the door to possibilities. Tonight, I was willing to take chances. What did I have to lose at this point? I had everything to gain. I was not going to let happiness pass me by this time. I had the confidence to seize what had always been just outside my reach. I was going to reap the goodness that I had sown throughout my life, as I was tired of reaping my father's shortcomings and always coming up wanting. The famine was over as far as I was concerned, and tonight I was stocking the food cellars of my soul.

There were other important dignitaries and nobles along with their daughters and sons at dinner. I was sat next to one of these boys. The only thing he seemed to be interested in was trying to stare down my dress. It was a smidgeon more revealing than what I was accustomed to, but not in a gaudy kind of way. Jordan was at the other end of the table across from me, beside his father. The young woman who was beside him was doing her best to impress herself upon him in a most obnoxious kind of way. I could see him trying to remain polite, but every time I glanced in his direction, I found him staring at me. He did not even seem the least bit apologetic about my catching him doing so. He would smile coyly and then redirect his attention back to his assigned guest. While dinner was quite delectable, I found I could not really eat much. I was too wound up about Jordan's secret proposal.

The call to the dance hall finally came, and I wanted to bolt from my spot at the table like a wild horse would break from danger. To my dismay the boy that sat next to me at dinner asked me for the first dance. I hated protocol more than anything right now. "Of course, I would be delighted to accept your invitation to dance," I said numbly.

The couples lined up on opposite sides of the dance floor and the music began its story. Normally I would have enjoyed this moment, and let the music carry me on its whim, but who I was dancing with brought me crashing hard to the ground over and over again. I was beyond even being able to carry on the simple banter of polite conversation with him. He finally noticed, and the song finished with us in silence.

I spent the next hour trying to get close to Jordan, but was always foiled by some young man. I would rather have a festering wound than to have to endure this type of attention for the next two years. *What have I gotten myself into? How can I possibly entertain these strangers who want my favor and attention? I have nothing to offer that is worthwhile other than a title and a possible kingdom. I guess that is reason enough for most.*

I was thirsty and headed over to the beverage table. I sensed someone approaching from behind me, and I heard him clear his throat. I muffled the groan that was rising, and turned with a look of apathy on my face. It was a good thing I did not have a glass in my hand, or I would have soiled my dress. He was stunningly handsome, tall, and very masculine. His blue eyes were like sapphires and I resisted the urge to touch him to make sure he was real.

"Princess Annaliessa, I would like to introduce myself and ask for your permission to speak with you for a few moments if I may?"

"You may," I answered, like I was going to say no.

"I am Alexander of Marcynth. My family trades with the kingdoms to the far north of our land."

"It is a pleasure to meet some one from Prince Charles' kingdom."

"I must tell you that you have gained quite a following among the people of all the kingdoms of our land. Your bravery, intellect, and compassion have not gone unnoticed."

"You flatter me, Alexander, but I do not like taking credit for doing what is good and right."

"I can see the people have not wasted their adoration then. You are humble as well. A trait not often found among royals."

"So I am told. Tell me, Alexander, what made you seek me out for this conversation?"

"I had heard you were pretty, but I fear the stories were far from truthful."

"How so?" I said a bit agitated.

"You are quite beautiful, actually. I imagine it will be hard for you to determine which man will be after your title or beauty, or both."

"I think the ideal man would be after neither."

"Yes, you have plainly declared you want to marry for love. Do you really see that as a possibility given the current circumstances?"

"It will be most arduous a task to weed out the fortune and power seekers, or those that just want to rule me physically, but I will make a gallant effort, I assure you." I happened to look up, just to my right, and saw Jordan with a look of anger on his face. Something had made him upset, but I was not sure what it was. He was surrounded by at least a dozen women, and he was trying to extricate himself from the bunch in a most abrupt fashion.

Alexander followed my gaze, and smiled. "It seems our short conversation has stirred the ire of the Prince."

"What makes you say that?"

"A man can always see the look of possessiveness on another man when it comes to a woman."

"Are you suggesting that Prince Jordan is jealous of our talking to each other?"

"Yes, that is exactly what I am saying."

Jordan was at my side a second later. "Princess Annaliessa, I hope you are not too tired to entertain a dance with me."

"I would be most delighted. Would you excuse me, Alexander? It was most pleasant to meet you. I found your conversation very entertaining, and hope I will have an opportunity to engage you in such again in the near future."

"I am a willing participant. All you have to do is ask, and I shall be at your service," he said with a wicked grin.

I felt Jordan take my arm and he very persuasively steered me as far away from Alexander as he could.

"What is wrong with you, Jordan?"

"I did not like the way he was looking at you."

"And how was that exactly?"

"I think you know what I mean, Annaliessa. He was practically undressing you with his eyes."

"My, you really have an overactive imagination, Jordan. The only person who was undressing me with their eyes tonight was the boy I sat next to at dinner. Did you not pick up on how he kept leaning over me to talk?"

"Yes, I noticed that, too, and I already spoke to him about how inappropriate his behavior was at the dinner table."

"You spoke to him?!"

"He was most remorseful after our talk."

"I cannot believe you. When did you have time to break free from the clutches of your admirers to chat with him?"

"You would be surprised what I can accomplish when I am motivated."

"How much longer do I have to endure the company of men who only want to look down my dress, or want my attention for the position they gain? I would much rather hear your proposal."

"I think I am getting quite tired. Do you feel a headache coming on, Annaliessa?"

"Now that you mention it, I do feel a bit of throbbing starting to creep in," I smiled with appreciation.

"I think perhaps you should give some polite excuse to my parents and get the rest you need."

"I will be retiring a short time after you have gone. I do not want to be too obvious."

"I will await your arrival at the secret passage to my room then."

"Yes, I will come for you. Annaliessa, do you like the dress?" he said as an afterthought.

"It is the most beautiful thing I have ever worn. Your generosity is most kind. I am actually reluctant to take it off."

The smile that crossed his face at that statement made me blush. Realizing I recognized the look on his face made him blush in return. In that moment, he truly looked so adorable, that my heart leapt in my chest, and I felt myself start to perspire. *I had better get myself to my room before I make a spectacle out of myself,* I thought.

Dangerous Possibilities

21

It was almost an hour before I heard the faint knock at the panel to the passage way. I rushed to it just as it slid open to reveal a repentant Jordan.

"I tried to get away sooner. Please forgive my tardiness. My father kept introducing me to people, and then the girls were incessant with their demands to be recognized. It was unbearable, I assure you."

I let out a giggle, "Shall we go to your special place and relax?"

"Definitely!"

It was a lovely night, and the stars were on display for our amusement. I felt the tension of the day fading from my body as I let my gaze span the horizon. Jordan was standing so close to me our arms were touching. I could feel him relax, but there was still the sense of readiness in his muscle, as if he was faced with a situation that caused for a quick reaction.

He turned to face me, and reached his hand up to my face, and used it to turn me so that I mirrored his position. He stood there staring at me for such a long time, his thumb stroking my cheek. I could have endured this attention all night, but I had to know what was on his mind.

"Jordan, please tell me what you had promised me earlier. I have reached my limit on the suspense, and I honestly cannot take another minute."

"Annaliessa, you know that I love you, I believe I made that clear earlier today."

"I know you did not bring me here, Jordan, just to tell me you love me again."

"No, but it is important for you to know it, so you know the motivation behind what I am proposing. I want to have you for my wife, and I think you will see that there is also a very practical purpose in our union as well, when I finish sharing my thoughts with you. I just wanted to make sure you did not hone in on the practical aspects as being the motivation behind what I say."

"Annaliessa, I have tried to deny the powerful pull you seem to have on my heart, but I no longer want to resist it. I wanted to be sure it was not the bonding causing the attraction I have felt grow for you year after year, but now that the bonding is broken, I have felt it grow even stronger, and I cannot contain the emotions that are coursing through my mind and my body any longer. Seeing another man leer at you through dinner and multiple men dancing with you was most excruciating. When Alexander approached you, I lost command of my emotions. I know the effect he has on women, and I could not risk him working his charms on you."

"Jordan, jealousy does not become you. If you are not confident in your qualities to attract and keep the attention of a woman, you will always struggle under its hand."

"There is only one woman I am interested in keeping entertained." He leaned down and took possession of my mouth.

It was hesitant and tender, like he was waiting for me to invite him to take more. I was so nervous, I did not want to repeat my mistakes with Tyson, and I did not want to lead Jordan on. I had no idea what the right thing was to do, but I, too, wanted to know if things were different from before, but was this the best moment to find out?

"Jordan," I said, backing away a bit from his kiss. "I think you had better share your proposal with me before you stray down this path of diversion."

He exhaled a breath of frustration, but said, "You are right. I had best speak my mind before I lose all train of intelligent reasoning, which is so easy to do when I am near you."

"Do not interrupt me before I finish," he scolded. "Annaliessa, I think it is actually in your best interest to marry a prince. Since your castle was destroyed in the earthquake, and the curse has been lifted by marrying outside of royal or noble lineages, have you thought about the possibilities it presents your father?"

"No, I am not sure I follow you."

"Since your father does not love your mother, would it be beneath him to find a way of disposing of her so he could marry another and have more children?"

I felt the air leave my lungs. Panic began to creep up and take hold of my body. Jordan pressed on with his proposal, I think in fear that he was losing me to the panic that must be visible on my face.

"If this happens, and you have married someone other than a prince with his own kingdom, you could find your life and that of your children in jeopardy should your father have a son to claim the throne of your kingdom. So, you see, if you are married to a prince, and by that I mean me, you will always have a kingdom and our child would be heir to this kingdom and not a threat to your father."

"Jordan, I believe what you say is true. My mother's life is very much in danger. As soon as the first prince ends up having more than one child, proving that the curse is ineffective, he will not hesitate to kill her. His greed and thirst for domination have exceeded the boundaries of all that is holy, good, and acceptable. He will stop at nothing to get it."

"Annaliessa, will you marry me?" The question was spoken lovingly, so much so, I could not deny his sincerity.

"Jordan, even though I agree with everything you just said, I cannot and will not marry you unless I am sure I love you. I do not doubt your sincerity in your feelings towards me, but I have to be sure I feel the same way. I will not curse you to a life without love. You deserve to have it, and I will not be the person to deny you receiving it. It would be far too painful to live if that was your fate."

"Annaliessa, it would be far too painful to live without you."

He drew me into an embrace and clung to me without shame. His hand brushed back the strands of my hair that barred him access to my neck, and his lips began to make a pathway from my ear to the base of my neck. *Oh dear, did he have any idea how splendid this felt?* It was exhilarating, and I felt the explosion of heat in the depth of my core. It was unfurling its tendrils and seeking to mate with the heat of another like it. He took my mouth and laid a claim to it like he had never done before. I could not stop what was happening. I wanted to know every inch of his warm, moist tongue. I wanted this moment seared into my memory so I could replay it over and over again, to analyze it for what it might really mean to me. I felt the shockwave of our heat connecting, and I knew he was ruining any opportunity for another man to claim my affections. His yearning had been penned up so long, that the ferociousness of it implored me to acquiesce to his petition for more. I returned the intensity of his kiss and knew I was on dangerous ground. I was about to head over the cliff, and he was following far too close to not get injured.

"Jordan, Jordan," I panted. "Please stop. You know this is not a good idea. Please, I do not want to hurt you. If you do not stop now you risk an injury I will be powerless to heal should things not work out how you hope."

"Annaliessa, it was far too late for that the moment you stepped foot into this castle. You own my heart, and it is forever yours to love or break."

The tears came then, and I sobbed into his shoulder as he held me to him. I would never be able to live up to his expectation of me. He was far too good for me. My father would somehow manage to destroy us and our happiness, but I wanted so urgently to believe we could have a happy ending. I sensed that someone or something was not going to let that happen, and my heart was breaking at the thought that I was going to lose him and there was nothing I could do to stop it.

He held me in his arms all night. I was never so disappointed that the sun had risen in all my life as I was the next morning. He kissed me tenderly before taking me back to my room so I could change and get ready for breakfast.

We spent the next two days in each other's company. He never overstepped the boundaries of proper courtship when we were chaperoned. However, each night, in our secret place, we grew closer together in friendship, and the flames of passion burned hotter. He was quite ardent in his quest to have me as his wife, and I was finding it harder to resist.

The Queen's Summons

22

I awoke to a persistent knocking at my bedroom door. I reluctantly cracked it open to see an agitated servant. "The Queen requests an audience with you immediately. I am to personally escort you, so I implore you to make haste in making yourself presentable."

"I understand. I'll put on a dress and brush my hair. It should only take a few minutes."

I closed the door and leaned against it. From the look on his face I was not sure my meeting with the queen was going to be as enjoyable as last time. I was anxious already, and I feared Jordan and I had been discovered in our attempt to spend time un-chaperoned. *How much trouble was I going to be in?*

I was practically pushed through the door of the queen's chambers, and the servant wasted no time in retreating. I do not recall ever seeing the queen in an unpleasant mood, so I could not help but dread what was coming.

"Annaliessa, I would like you to tell me where you were last night well past dark. Do not insult me by saying you were in your bed sleeping, as I know for a fact you were not there, and my son was not in his bed either."

"Your Majesty, I would not lie to you. I respect you too much to do you the dishonor. I was with Jordan."

"When did you return to your room?"

"This morning at sunrise," I said with my eyes focused on a spot on the floor.

"You spent the entire night with my son, without any chaperone. Is that correct?"

"Yes, Your Majesty, but it is not for what you are thinking."

"Your maiden's virtue has not been compromised in any fashion, Annaliessa?"

"Queen Sarah, your son is, and always has been a gentleman where I am concerned. He has not tarnished himself or his family in that manner. We have just been talking. It is hard to talk openly when there are extra sets of ears present."

"Have you spoken to Jordan already? Surely he has given you the same report."

"He did confess the same story you are telling me now, but how do I know the two of you did not discuss this in the event that you were caught?"

I think the look of shock that hung on my face spoke for me. "We have done nothing to be ashamed of, so I do not see the need for pretenses."

"Tell me, Annaliessa, have you figured out the answers to the matters we discussed previously?"

"Are you asking me if I love your son?"

"Yes, that is exactly what I am asking."

"I find his company to be very enjoyable, and our friendship has grown stronger and deeper, but if I am pressed for an answer this very moment, I do not have one to give beyond what I just expressed."

"We are expecting the arrival of a cousin imminently, so I will not send you home just yet. I know where the two of you have been spending your time, so I trust that you will refrain from visiting it again while you are here."

"I give you my word that I will not meet him there again."

"We will be throwing a small party this evening. I will be checking your room tonight as well, so I expect to find you in your bed when I do. Is that understood?"

"I know what you expect of me, Your Majesty. I will not disappoint you."

"Annaliessa, if you do not know how you feel towards my son by now, I would request you take some time at home to figure it out after this evening's festivities."

"I intend to take some time to explore that very topic today. If I need more time, I will leave tomorrow, so as not to cause any misunderstandings."

"Very well, you are dismissed."

I bowed and left the room. I can only imagine the exchange that took place between Jordan and his mother. I did not even think to ask if the king had knowledge of this indiscretion. I certainly hoped she was keeping it to herself. I did not want to entertain what my reception at home would be like if word got to my father. I only know it would be very painful indeed.

A Small Affair

23

B rian, the prince's cousin arrived a couple of hours later. He was older than Jordan at twenty and five years. It was a surprise to discover he was unmarried. How he managed to escape the duties of producing heirs to this point was scandalous based on the gossip I was hearing around the castle. He was apparently well-known for his prowess with the women, and I was warned to keep my guard. What he lacked in looks he made up for in charm. Not that he was ugly. He was average looking, around six feet tall, with brown hair and eyes that matched. He had a strong nose, round face and sported a well-manicured goatee. Charming, yes, he was no stranger in the ways to extend compliments and had everyone enraptured with his stories. He was particularly keen on keeping me entertained, and I saw the strain on Jordan's face as he maintained the aloofness that was now expected where the two of us were concerned.

Brian sensed the tension as well, but was able to ignore it brilliantly. In spite of it, we were all laughing at his tales of travel and intrigue. *Yes, it was a wonder this man was not married, but I was sure that was exactly the way he wanted it.*

Jordan was called away to attend to some business for the kingdom and I found myself enjoying a more intimate one-on-one conversation with Brian.

"Princess Annaliessa, has my cousin proposed marriage to you yet?"

I think the shade of red I was turning was enough of a reply.

"I think, based on your reaction that he most certainly has. Has he been bold enough to kiss you yet? If I were him, I definitely would risk the scandal to taste your delicate kisses."

"I see the reputation you have garnered is well deserved."

"You have not agreed to marry him though, have you?"

"No. I have been trying to determine if he would be better off without me. He did present a valid retort to my suggestion that he should seek other affections than mine. He was most persuasive."

"I think you will have to share this plan with me at dinner, and I will share my insights with you as well. You may not have asked for my opinion, but when it comes to love, I just cannot help myself, that is when it involves the love of someone other than me," he smiled sheepishly and then bowed as he bid me farewell until dinner.

Dinner was a smaller affair than the first ball, but still rather well-attended. I was sat between Alexander of Marcynth and Brian. Jordan as always, was seated at the opposite end by his parents. They had him flanked by two very beautiful women, and I felt as if I was being reprimanded all over again. I know it was wrong of me to think the queen had arranged the seating this way to show me my place when it came to the overstepping of bounds with her son, but I just could not help it. It stung.

Alexander was most grateful for the seating arrangement and he sent defiant looks in Jordan's direction. He kept me engaged in conversation throughout most of dinner. Brian tried to take the lead in the conversation several times, but Alexander was skilled in maneuvering it back to where he wanted it to go.

"Princess Annaliessa, I would very much like to accompany you to the dance floor this evening," Alexander stated. "I did not have the opportunity to do so the last time we met, and I would like to demonstrate my skill under your adept tutelage."

"You flatter me more that I deserve, Alexander, but Brian had asked me earlier today if he could have the first couple of dances, and I agreed."

Brian, astute as he was, heartily chimed in. "Yes, I could not resist such a beautiful young woman as the princess. She has been the most welcoming and amiable company I have come across in some time. I see you are agreeable on this account of her character."

"Yes, quite so," said Alexander in a less than genial way. "May I request the next couple of dances afterward, Your Highness?"

I did not want to dance with either of them, but I had to be courteous. I was under acute scrutiny this evening, and I was bound to play my part.

"Alexander, I would be most delighted to share the dance floor with you this evening."

Before I knew it, dinner was over and it was time for the real diplomacy to begin.

Brian took me straight to the dance floor and wasted no time in ascertaining what his cousin had proposed that I found so intriguing. He was surprised by what I shared and found an opportunity to slide off the dance floor and around an alcove where he could talk to me more privately.

I was nervous, as the last thing I needed was for Queen Sarah to notice my absence and find me alone with yet another male family member.

At least Jordan was otherwise distracted at the moment with his dance partner, or at least I hoped so. After the last exchange between Jordan and Alexander, I did not want to have to referee any further territorial disputes where I was concerned. It was completely insane that I was even thinking like this. A moon cycle ago, I would have never imagined I would be in this position, and I was still uncomfortable with it.

Twisted Fate

24

I told Brian about how Jordan felt it was best if we were married, and that I tended to agree with him. There was also the fact that he loved me, and I was beginning to think that I loved him, too, and probably always had; I just did not realize it before. I had bought the lie about it being some kind of special feeling.

"Annaliessa, on the surface that does seem like the best course of action, but I have to ask you if you really think that Tyson will remove the curse from your father?"

"What do you mean, Brian? Do you really think that is possible?"

"He wants revenge, Annaliessa, and you are a key component in that revenge. If you marry a prince you will automatically fall under the headship of that kingdom. If he cannot have any other heirs to pass his kingdom to, he will lose his place of power. You know that your father will not allow that to happen. He will invade the kingdom you have merged with and he will not stop until he has killed you and our prince. This is especially true given the destruction of your castle. Then two kingdoms will suffer, not just one. Your father will gain control over both kingdoms and rule them through your child. Vulterrian is the most vulnerable kingdom because the king and queen married for love, and they will not leave each other and marry another to have more children, like the other kings might. With only one heir, it puts them at risk to be taken over if anything happens to my cousin."

"Brian, you have given voice to my worst fears. That I would lose the one I love to the wicked striving for gain of my father. I could not bear to live if that happened, and the thought of my father getting his hooks into my child and blackening his or her heart with his malevolent control, makes me quiver with terror."

Jordan rounded the corner just then, and he did not look hospitable toward Brian at all. In fact, he had that jealous overprotective shroud on that was becoming easier for me to detect. He really looked like he wanted to physically remove his cousin from my vicinity.

"Cousin, exactly what are your intentions in taking my guest away from the dance?" Jordan asked the question with a smile on his face, but it was anything but friendly.

"We were just discussing kingdom business, and the possible merger of two of them being under consideration," I said sweetly. I felt sick and I did not want Jordan to know how close all our happiness was to being laid to waste.

"I think you owe me a dance, Annaliessa," Jordan stated with the purpose of taking me back to the ballroom.

"Unfortunately, Prince Jordan, I must add you to my dance card for a later point in the evening, as the next couple of dances belong to Alexander."

I heard the distinct sound of Jordan gritting his teeth. He smiled for his cousin's benefit, but he was barely controlling his hostility toward Alexander and his advances toward me.

"Well I would not want to keep any young man waiting for their opportunity to dance with you, Princess."

The sarcasm was dripping from his lips, and I could not help but giggle at how upset he was. This did not endear me to him at that moment. If I did not know how he felt about me, I might be a bit concerned at the glare he directed toward me.

I was hardly in the mood to entertain anyone. I just wanted to be alone with my thoughts. *I have to come up with a plan to ensure we will all be safe, and that my father never manages to get what he wants.* Tyson would have to be part of it, if I had any hope of living a long life with Jordan. He was the key to stopping my father in his tracks, and I knew it was going to cost me more than I really wanted to pay.

New Plan

25

Since I was not going to be able to meet Jordan in our special spot tonight, I took the next couple of hours to form a plan as I lay on my bed.

The main goal was to ensure that my father could under no circumstance have any more children, and if this meant a new curse that was applicable to him alone, I was all for it. He had no business being a father, and I could say that better than anyone.

If I could also guarantee that the other royals could have children without having to marry commoners, then no one else would have to die in the legal pursuit to remarry and reproduce. So far, I saw this as a win-win for everyone.

The kingdoms would remain free of my father's dominance and there would never be a shortage of marriageable offspring.

The one problem is that I know the only thing I have to bargain with is me. There is nothing better to offer Tyson to get the revenge he is seeking than to offer him the one thing he lost and may still want.

I was going to offer him my maiden's virtue and give him a child. I was not going to marry him, as I am not willing to give him the title of King or a throne of any kind. I would only be trading one reign of terror for another. This gave him the ultimate revenge: the shaming of the king's daughter, a king who could not further his own lineage, and the benefit of a child of his own. I was truly mournful about the fact that there would be no way any man, let alone Jordan, would marry me after bearing another man's child out of wedlock. My kingdom would be bereft of heirs as a result. *Perhaps with a child, Tyson would soften his heart once again, and be the young man I knew was possible. If only he could release the hate and leave revenge behind. Maybe he would grow to love me, or at the very least not despise me, and I could at least have the same degree of happiness that most of the other royals lived with.* Somehow, it was just going to have to be enough.

I called out to Evirent in my mind and told him that I would need him tomorrow for a most important and dangerous kingdom errand. I would leave in the morning and have Evirent take me to Tyson before I could change my mind. It was probably a good thing I could not see Jordan tonight. I was uncertain if I could remain silent about my plan, nor could I trust myself to not wilt under his touch, and be selfish regardless of the costs. Evirent's reply rippled through my mind, *"Just let me know where, and I will be ready to assist you in your task."*

I heard my door open and the queen step inside. She walked over to my bed to ensure I was actually occupying it. I had put my nightdress on earlier and pretended to be asleep. She did not need to know that I was lying awake contemplating the bleak future I was about to embark on. She would try to stop me because it would bring pain to her son. No, as far as she was concerned, I was sound asleep indeed.

Surprise Visit

26

It was already very late by the time the queen had come in for the bed check. I was totally surprised when a half hour later, the panel in my room slid open and there stood Jordan with a couple of blankets draped over his shoulders, an oil lamp in his hand and an impish grin on his countenance.

"Grab your slippers. We are going for a walk," he whispered. "Jordan, your mother may do another bed check, and I am certain that she has someone stationed at our special spot."

"Hence the reason we are going somewhere else. You can stay here if you want, but I am really hoping you will join me."

I knew I should say no, but this was likely going to be the last happy moment I was going to have for the remainder of my life, so I was willing to be ill-behaved and throw caution to the wind. "I just need to put something else on, as I am in my nightdress."

"No one is going to see us, Annaliessa, and we do not have the time to waste if we are going to make it to our destination undetected."

I tossed back the covers and slid into my slippers. I grabbed his hand and he practically dragged me to the secret passage. We took a different passage than what had become our familiar one.

It went down for what seemed like forever. We came to a tunnel and made our way down it at a fairly brisk pace. We reached the end and came to a door that was locked. He pressed some rocks on the wall and a storage compartment was revealed. He took out the key and put it in the lock, and with a full turn of the key, the lock released its hold.

"When we step out to the path on the cliff, you need to press yourself as close as you can to the rock face to ensure that you are not seen. When we are far enough down the path I will let you know and then we can walk down without fear of being discovered. Here is a blanket. Wrap it around you as the wind will most likely be strong and you will be cold."

I did as instructed. He wrapped the other blanket around himself, and he pried open the door slightly and peeked out. He seemed to feel secure that we could exit so he slipped through the narrow opening, pulling me immediately behind him. The wind was strong and the chill it produced brought goose flesh to my skin, and my teeth started to chatter seconds later. If it was not for the fact that half my body surface was plastered to the rock face protecting it from the wind, I would have frozen instantly. We shimmied down the slanted path for a couple hundred feet. With no oil lamp to guide us out here, I hoped he knew the path well enough in the dark as to keep us from injury.

I was starting to wonder just how long this path was and how long we would have to continue in this manner, when he turned to face me. The wind buffeted him and pulled his nightshirt taut against his body. I was treated to every luscious muscle on his body in stark definition. I was unable to pull my eyes away from his manhood, as it was obvious he was naked under his shirt, as I was under mine. I would have blushed if it were not for the fact that I was freezing.

He motioned for me to take his hand, and I stepped away from the rock face and braced myself for the wind that would hit my back. He turned and led me down the rest of the path to a beach. Normally, letting the sand squish through my toes would have been delightful, but I was far too cold to relish it. There was a sand bar in front of us, and it helped to act as a windbreaker. "Just a little further and we will be to our destination."

There was a small cave-like structure built into the sand which offered some privacy and protection from the elements. Once inside, he laid his blanket on the sand, sat upon it, and invited me to join him. I did not hesitate, as I wanted warmth more than anything at this moment. I sat next to him and wrapped the blanket I had around us both.

"I am sorry I had to be so secretive and spontaneous about our meeting tonight, but there was no way I was not going to see you," he said as he turned to look at me.

"You do not need to be sorry. I was struggling with the idea of spending the night without your company. It seems I have become accustomed to it, and have found it most enjoyable."

"I need you, Annaliessa. I no longer feel complete without you by my side. It is as if the most important part of me is missing when you are not near, and it feels like torture to see you with some one else."

I was on dangerous ground at this point, and I knew everything I planned was riding on my remaining resolute even when he was melting every wall of resistance I had tried to build to ensure I would be able to carry on with my plan.

"Jordan, you have nothing to fear from another man. My heart no longer seeks fulfillment or happiness with anyone else. It is set on you, and regardless of what fate brings us; that will never change, at least not for me."

"Annaliessa, that sounds like a declaration of love. Have I misunderstood you, or are you really saying that you love me?"

"You know how I feel about misunderstandings, so perhaps my kiss will relate to you my heart's desire." I leaned into him and placed my hand on his chest and ran it up to his neck so I could pull him to me.

He did not resist and met my mouth with the full anticipation of complete access. He was not disappointed. Our tongues slipped effortlessly over each other's and danced to the beat of our hearts. He shifted, but did not break the kiss that was deepening in desire. He was on his knees and pulling me to his tight chest. Our night clothes protected nothing, and I was introduced to the full measure of his erection. My mind was racing and I found my own body responding in a way I was powerless to hide. It was so much more than just the coming together of two people in a sexual way that I was reacting to. I wanted to be joined to him completely, physically, emotionally, and spiritually. I wanted the consummation of our love to be tied to my soul forever, as it was the only solace I would have in the future. I knew this was selfish of me, as it might affect his ability to unite satisfactorily with another woman, but right now, I was not feeling generous or thoughtful of others. I was possessed by a need for comfort, and a yearning to know him in the fullest of senses. I had never craved anything as much as I wanted him now, and I was ravenous for his touch, for his love.

He pulled his mouth away from mine only to take it on a tour down my neck. He shifted his weight once again, and I found myself being laid down onto my back with him pressed up against me. He had his engorged manhood pressed against my hip, and one leg was between my own. I felt the moisture gathering between my legs in an effort to welcome him in. The throbbing sensation was beginning to take control, and I could not abstain from thinking about what it would feel like to have him fully inside me. I became conscious of the fact that his hand had found purchase on my breast and his fingers were nimbly drawing my nipple to full attention. It was like my body was operating without any instigation on my part, and I felt my hips rise to meet him. I took the fullness of his instrument of pleasure into my hand and heard him growl with a lusty moan.

Without warning he pulled himself away from me. "Annaliessa, stop! My self-control is hanging by a thread and if you persist, I will not be able to keep myself from taking what is not rightfully mine to claim just yet."

"Jordan, you want to be righteous and honorable now?"

If he knew what I was planning to do in the morning, he would not hesitate to take what I was offering at this moment. I wanted to know the experience of having this man whom I loved and who loved me in return, make love to me before I had to experience it in a less than ideal way with Tyson.

"It may be trivial to hold back given where we are and how far we have already gone, but I am still quite traditional, and I want to honor you the way you should be honored. To violate that now would rob both of us of the joy of our wedding night. Besides, I am already distraught at the thought of not being with you every night as we have been. I cannot imagine the excruciating sense of loss if I claim what is not legally mine to have, but that which I would burn even hotter for."

"I admire your sense of honor and duty, Jordan, but choosing to exercise it at this moment is wrecking havoc on my mind and body."

"Just so we are clear, it is killing me as well. The blaze of passion you have ignited in my loins and in my soul is causing me to question just how badly I want to cling to honor and righteousness."

"I think it is best if I go back home tomorrow, Jordan. This turmoil is too powerful to ignore, and I cannot exercise enough strength to hold it back any longer."

"Then I suggest you accept my proposal and marry me soon, very soon."

"I am not sure our marriage will meet with our parent's approval. What will you do if they object to our union?" *I knew this entire conversation was moot, but I could not let on to my plan. I needed him to believe I was leaving solely because of temptation, which was also a valid reason at this moment.*

"You have reason to believe there would be a dissention to our unification?"

"You know how unpredictable my father can be. What if he insists that I marry someone other than a prince?"

"I am not above kidnapping you and secretly marrying you in another land if I have to. Annaliessa, I will not let anything get in the way of our being together forever."

The tears trickled down my checks, and I recognized my heart was beginning to mourn what I was about to have ripped away from me. It was most acute. I wanted to sob bitterly, but I could not give in to the emotion or he would know that something was wrong.

"Why are you crying Annaliessa? Is what I said distressing to you in some way?"

Yes, was the answer ringing through my head, but I quietly said, "It was such a sweet thing to say, and I was overcome with such emotion by it. Do not worry, my love. I am sorry if my tears upset you." Before he could respond, I drew his mouth to mine and kissed him like it was the last time I would ever do so, and in reality, it was.

I was regretting my sense of duty and honor to the lives of others. Jordan did not have the exclusive market on this attribute, even though I was behaving rather aberrant right now lying here next to him and craving his touch. My appetite to satisfy this coveting of his body was like a starving lioness hunting her prey. Instinct was driving my need to feast on the delicacies of his body and controlling the lustful longing of my awakened hunger was all that mattered. Jordan, always the champion of what is good and pure, ensured that I did not succumb.

It was still dark when we made our way back to the castle. I let him lead me back to my room, and kissed him one last time.

I fell into my bed and cried for the remaining hours to dawn.

The Offering

27

I got dressed just before sunrise and packed my things. I left a note on my dressing table for Jordan. I needed him to understand why I was doing this. I wanted him to know how much I loved him and how much this was rending my heart. I knew this would catch his attention, as parchment for writing was extremely costly, and only royals and clergy were privy to it.

I sent a mental message to Evirent to meet me at the beach where I had spent several of the most intimate and memorable hours of my life. I went through the passage, and thankfully remembered how to open the storage compartment for the key to the door. I travelled down the same path I had taken the previous night with Jordan. Evirent arrived a moment later. I shared with him what I was planning to do, and he warned me not to trust Tyson to abide by the terms of any agreement I was proposing. In fact, he was reluctant to aid me at all, but he was an honorable creature as well, and carried me to my destination without another word.

It was still dark when he left me in the woods by the willow tree. I turned to make my way toward Joseph and Maria's place. I did not get more than a few steps when Tyson called to me from behind the tree. I stopped in my tracks and turned to find him standing there with his arms crossed over his chest.

"My mother came to me in a dream last night telling me you were coming to meet me here. Annaliessa, what brings you out to the woods unescorted? Have you run away from home?"

"That would be a more pleasant excuse than the truth of why I am here."

"What could possibly bring you to risk your life in coming to see me alone? Does anyone know you are here? Does Prince Jordan know you are here? I have heard how you have been spending a great deal of time with him, and how possessive of you he is."

"Gossip is always quick to circulate; the truth, on the other hand, takes more time."

"You are denying the rumors then?"

"I am just saying that gossip can sometimes carry a bit of truth, but it usually has been embellished with a lie."

"Enough pleasantries, what has brought you here to meet me, Annaliessa?"

"I have a plan that will gratify your need for revenge and quench other needs as well."

"I am all ears. Please enlighten me."

"I do not want my father to be able to have any other children. You know it is not beneath him to rid himself of my mother and marry a commoner to get sons to secede him. They will be raised to be as ruthless as he, and I cannot bear to see the people suffer under his hand any longer than is necessary. I know you have the magic necessary to exempt the curse completely from all the royals, which includes me, and leave it in place for my father, and that is what I am asking you to do."

"You want me to release you and the other royals so they can have more children with each other, and not just commoners, but put an exclusive curse on your father so that he cannot bear another child.

Does this mean you want your mother set free from the curse as well, or would she be bound to your father's fate?"

"I want her free from the curse as well as the others. Should my father try to rid himself of my mother, I want him to be unable to further his plague of control and manipulation."

"That is a very bold request, Annaliessa. What could you possibly offer me in return to even tempt me to do what you suggest?"

"I will give you my maiden's virtue and bear you a child. You will have the revenge you want against my father by ensuring his reign will come to an end, and you will have shamed me by lying with me and conceiving a child out of wedlock, ensuring no man will ever desire me for a wife. As a result, your child will be the only one I will bear."

"How would I know that you would not kill me after I have planted my seed within you? How can I be sure I will live to raise this child?"

"It will not be by my hand that you will die. You have magic to aid you in your protection, so why are you posing this issue?"

"I just know that my mother died a slow and painful death at your father's hand, and she had magic."

"I can only offer you what I have control over. Your fate is your own matter to work out. I do not wish you dead. I am not my father. Do we need to have this discussion again? Besides, I am in more danger of dying before or after the baby is born than you. I will have two men wanting me dead, you and my father. I should be asking you to ensure that I will live, not the other way around."

"I agree to your proposal and your terms, Annaliessa. However, I am bound by the terms of the spell and they require a new moon which will not be for another two days.

"I will take you to where I have been staying since we last saw each other. I left Joseph and Maria's after our last exchange. I promise you will remain unharmed until we complete our business."

"It seems I have very little option, as I do not want anyone knowing that I am here. Lead the way."

The Letter

28

I awoke rather late the next morning. My first thoughts were of Annaliessa and the few hours we spent together in the cave at the beach. I had wanted to take her so desperately last night, to know what it would feel like to be one with her, and to make her feel happy and replete with the joys of making love. It was so difficult to back off when she was practically beseeching me to do so. I knew our wedding night was going to be idyllic. I just had to ask her father for her hand in marriage. It was a task that was going to be rather unpleasant, but she was worth it. I wanted to head off to see her father today, and we could travel together, thus allowing me even more time with her.

I jumped out of bed in a hurry to dress and tell her of my plan. The castle was fully awake, and it seemed silly to use the secret passage way, but it felt strange to visit her any other way. I headed down the now well-known passage way to her room and slid the panel open without knocking. I figured we had very little secrets between us at this point, so knocking was not necessary.

I was stunned to find the room empty. All her things were gone, and there was a note addressed to me on the dressing table. It felt like I was going in slow motion, as if in a dream. I took the note into my shaking hand and opened it with a sick feeling rising in my stomach.

My dearest Jordan,

I am sorry I left without saying good-bye, but there was a matter of most urgency for all our sakes that I must attend to. I could not tell you last night, as I knew you would try to stop me from what must be done to ensure everyone's happiness, and for some of us, our lives.

My desire is to be your wife, and to live with you for the rest of my life. I am afraid that after I have fulfilled my task, you will no longer wish to have me as such. That is why my behavior last night was so brazen. I feared it was the last time I would feel the warmth of your embrace, and the passion of your kiss.

I pray that some day you will be able to forgive me for what I am about to do, but know that I did it with everyone's best interest at heart. The reign of injustice is about to end, and everyone will be free at last to enjoy their lives unfettered by any curse; well everyone but my father.

I will love you until my dying breath. My heart is yours forever.

Annaliessa

My lungs tried to draw breath, but it was as if there was no air with which I could fill them. I felt as if I was being choked by an invisible assailant. Dread began to flow through my body. My heartbeat raced, as though I had just been in a fight and lost. I was aching all over and panic was starting to become a familiar comrade.

I raced to my father's study, where I knew he would be during this time of day and burst through the doors, not waiting for the proper introduction.

My father took one look at me and knew there was nothing else more important than whatever had me in such an agitated state.

"She left, and she is going to do something very bad, and I know it involves Tyson and the curse. You have to help me find her before it is too late!" I screamed.

"Jordan, please calm down.

"Her letter said it is something to ensure everyone's happiness. Well, everyone except her father. She said that after it is done, I will no longer want her for my wife. She is risking far too much to end this curse. We already had a way around it. Why would she feel she needs to make sure it is totally eradicated? I do not understand, and I need to stop her!"

I had not noticed my cousin, Brian, sitting off to the side of the room until he spoke. "Perhaps I can help enlighten you on what the princess plans to do."

My father and I looked at him with astonishment. "Please, Brian, tell us what you know."

I had to sit down upon hearing what Brian shared with us. My world was crumbling all around me, and I was staggered by the debris it was leaving in its wake.

"How could she have gotten out of the castle without anyone seeing her?" I asked.

"Brian, would you mind giving me some time alone with my son. Please let the guards know that nothing or no one is to disturb us until I say otherwise."

"Yes, Your Majesty, right away." With that he rose and headed out the door.

I was angry with him for planting the thoughts in Annaliessa's head about this quest she was now on. I had every intention of letting him know exactly how angry I was as soon as I knew how to stop her from being harmed.

Bloodshed

29

"Jordan, what I am about to tell you, only three people know: your mother and I, and a friend that is like a brother to me, and now, you. You need to listen to the whole story without interrupting me. You may ask your questions after I am through, do you understand?"

"Yes, do not hold me in suspense any longer. I can barely hold myself together given the stress I feel right now."

"When your mother carried you in her womb, there was a complication. She had contracted a grave illness, and was dying, when she was just seven moon cycles along with child. Her struggle with the illness was only magnified given that she was fighting to keep both of you alive. She could not risk simply living if it meant losing you, as she would not be able to bear another child. The curse was in its infancy at that point, only having been placed upon the land that past sun's zenith. Annaliessa had just turned one year when your mother came down with the illness, and apparently her parents had been unsuccessful in trying for another child after the curse was pronounced. The validity of the curse was a source of great distress for us all, but more so for your mother and I."

"Given the seriousness of what was at stake, a friend of mine, whom shall remain anonymous, told me a most fascinating tale, and a way to save both of you. I, of course, was willing to do anything to ensure you both lived, just as you are now, to save Annaliessa from a horrible tragedy."

"Long ago, dragons ruled this land. They were the true nobility of this area. They were worshipped by the natives that had been here, and they had a peaceful co-existence with these natives. When previous adventurers came to this land, they saw it was desirable to possess, and they killed many of the dragons as well as the natives in order to plunder and keep the spoils to themselves."

"Our ancestors were some of the last to arrive. We were driven from our homeland by famine and disease, and few of us made the journey here without perishing."

"One of our kings was out on an expedition of the area that is now our kingdom, and he saw a dragon being attacked by an army of men. The dragon was pinned down with chains and had swords and spears being hurled at it, as the men could not get too close or risk being consumed by the fire that the dragon breathed. It was a young dragon and he took pity on it. He took his army of men and slaughtered the men that were attacking it and set it free. In return the dragon promised to help him gain control of the land if he would live in harmony with the dragons and let them live in peace."

"The king, being wise, saw that this alliance would be beneficial to our people. Who better to rid us of enemies and protect us than the dragons who ruled this land? We helped them drive out the other invaders and took in the natives, who blended into our numbers, and we became strong. The founding six families became the kingdoms you know today. Each family has a dragon that looks out for it and keeps the family safe, as long as we remain pure in heart."

"Annaliessa, as you know, has met such a dragon. In fact, he is the new dragon king, and he chose Annaliessa specifically to protect.

Evirent aided Annaliessa in leaving here and took her where she asked to go. I found out about it an hour ago when Cassia, our dragon, told me of what was to happen. You verified what she spoke about Annaliessa. I had no idea Brian had a part in this plan until now."

"Evirent is very distressed over this plan, and does not want Annaliessa to carry it out. He is very concerned about how this plan could upset the balance in our kingdoms and destroy our alliance. They will not let another man bent on destruction come to power, and Tyson is a most dangerous adversary, given his magical abilities. The beast that rages inside him cannot be let loose."

"Evirent has notified all the kings by way of the dragon protectors. We want to send you to Annaliessa's father and have you persuade him to make things right with Tyson so that Annaliessa does not have to sacrifice herself to save the kingdoms from his greed and stupidity. You will have the backing of all the other kingdoms and dragons as well. If King Claude does not do as we ask, he will be arrested and put to death for his crimes. This should appease Tyson and spare Annaliessa, but time is short, so the dragons will take a contingent from each kingdom's army with you as you need to leave immediately."

"Now, back to how this fits in with your mother. You need to know why you and Annaliessa are so important, and why the dragons will do anything to accomplish a beneficial outcome for us all."

"The only way to save your mother and you was through magic, but not just any magic. It had to be old and very pure magic to ensure you would live and be healthy, without damage. The only magic that pure and powerful was that which is contained in the blood of dragons. Evirent offered your mother and me this gift because we married for love and had good hearts. He would not have done it for any of the other royal couples."

"Your mother drank the blood and she recovered from the illness, and you were born healthy and strong. You have dragon's blood flowing through your veins, and therefore, they are very particular about who you marry. They were most pleased with your declaration of love for Annaliessa at such a young age, as she is pure in heart, and wishes to marry for love as well. These are the characteristics that ensure we will be able to live in harmony with the dragons. They loathe killing humans since they have promised to protect us, but King Claude crossed the line when he killed the dragon to paint Leah's prison cell with its blood. If it was not for the curse, they would have killed him long ago, but they have waited to see if Annaliessa would be the advocate they knew her to be, and if she would defend the cause of the helpless, stand in the face of injustice, and be willing to lay down her life to protect what is right and good. She has proven herself to be that and more and they will no longer sit back and watch, but will dole out the justice King Claude has had coming for many years. They do not want her harmed, and if this is not stopped, the damage could be irreparable."

"So you are saying that we all have some special link to the dragons, but I have a greater link because of what happened with my mother?"

"Yes, that is correct."

"Annaliessa is special to them as well because of her connection to me?"

"Yes and no. They have been particularly interested in Annaliessa, because of her key to the curse, being the only female. With the bonding that had been in place, they could not be sure she would marry for love, nor whether she would remain pure and humble, and would put others before herself. They wanted her to be united with someone as strong and noble in spirit as herself. You are that person. It is your blood that has drawn you to her from childhood. You would always be attracted to what is naturally pure of heart, and given that Annaliessa has remained such, you have grown more enamored with her every year. Once the bonding was broken, you were no longer restrained by the other four prince's claim on her heart, and your attachment to her grew exponentially. I cannot tell you that I understand how it all really works, but what it comes down to is that the two of you were meant to be together forever.

Your hearts cannot deny the goodness that connects you to each other in ways that go beyond any human knowledge. That kind of love is worth fighting for, worth dying for."

"So, how is it that you have been able to arrange this plan with the dragons and the other kings to deal with King Claude so quickly?"

"We have a mental connection with the dragons. They can communicate with our minds and we with theirs. We have all been sharing ideas and plans throughout the past hour, and now it is time to put everything into motion. The new moon is two days away, and I am told that is what the young warlock will need to release the curse completely. If we have not stopped Annaliessa from carrying out her plan by that time…well, I do not want to think about the repercussions. Son, you do understand she is offering herself to Tyson in exchange for everyone's freedom, right?"

"I do not know how I would live if she dies, father. I have to be successful."

"Jordan, she isn't offering him her life. She is offering him a child."

The revulsion gripped me tight and I let out a tortured scream I could not contain. It ripped through my body and tore my lungs to shreds before I exhausted myself from the effort. I finally understood why she wanted to be with me so desperately last night. *How stupid am I? She was offering me the one thing I had always wanted, her, and I said no. She knew what she was going to do last night, and she wanted to give me her maiden's virtue before Tyson took it from her, most likely by force. I could not bear the thought of him taking what did not belong to him, and hurting her while doing it.*

I struggled to remain upright, as I thought of what she must be going through and would endure at his hand all for others. Pure of heart, no, I was nowhere near pure in my thoughts or in my heart right now. I was bent on consuming everything and everyone in my way of getting to my love, my betrothed. I intended to exercise wrath on whatever stood before my path and blocked me from rescuing her and making her my wife. I was not going to wait for the proper etiquette to be performed this time. I was going to marry her immediately, and I did not care what anyone said, or the scandal it may cause.

"Son, I know this news is troubling you immensely, but you have to go now and do as I have instructed you. Evirent will help you find Annaliessa. He has been trying to connect with her, but he is sure Tyson is somehow blocking his ability to communicate with her. He does not know yet where she is, but he will find her and get you to her. Evirent had not expected to have this much difficulty in finding her, or he never would have let her go."

"I hope you are right, father. I hope he finds her before it is too late."

Sentencing

30

The other dragons and I carried the knights to Petroset. Each prince was in attendance, and they all carried grave looks to match the occasion. I was glad the day had finally come to put King Claude in his place. He had ruled with an iron fist for far too long, and I was glad to be one of the instruments of justice. I sympathized with Prince Jordan's plight. All of us dragons liked Annaliessa and had strong feelings of respect and friendship for her, and would do whatever we could to see her in the position of authority she deserved in her kingdom. All the kingdoms would be better off if she ruled the throne of Petroset.

¥

King Claude was surprised when contingents from every Kingdom arrived at his home. I entered and told him why we had all come. He held his daughter's fate in his hands and we were here to ensure he realized the significance of what was at risk. I was not surprised when he refused to aid his daughter. He threatened to not only kill me but everyone who had come with me. I assured him that I did not just come with an army of men, but I had the dragons backing me as well. This caused the color to drain from his face. He knew he was not going to wiggle out of this predicament. After all, he was the author of this particular story, but he no longer controlled the ending. We were about to set this drama in a new direction and let justice and righteousness strike a new tale.

King Claude was read his list of crimes and sentence was pronounced. He would be executed once we found Annaliessa. We knew Tyson would want to see it with his own eyes if he was going to relent and let Annaliessa go free from her commitment. In fact, we were certain he would want to be the executioner.

King Claude was taken to the prison and a dragon was stationed nearby as well as an army of men. He had no hope of escape, and he was allowed no visitors.

The only person I thought might want to visit him would be Queen Amanda, but she looked relieved that he was no longer going to be able to hurt her, Annaliessa, or anyone else anymore, and said she had nothing she needed to say to him except good riddance. This brought a smile of satisfaction to all of us, but to me especially. Of course, it only lasted a few seconds. I still had no idea where Annaliessa was and the new moon was tomorrow. Evirent had sent dragons scouring the kingdoms looking for any sign of the princess or the warlock, and none could be found. Tyson was far more skilled at the art of deception than I had given him credit for.

I could comprehend the dedication Tyson harbored in his thirst for revenge. The feelings related to revenge were as strong as those of love. I could appreciate him stopping at nothing to get what he desired, and I empathized with him, as I had an equally strong motivation to protect the one I loved.

At this point, sleep was a stranger. It was better if I did not close my eyes anyway, as the nightmarish images that played through my mind when I did kept me on the brink of losing my sanity. I had to maintain control; breaking down would not help Annaliessa. I had to stay focused and stay positive, but every minute that passed made it all the harder to keep lunacy at bay.

New Moon Rising

31

It was the longest two days of my life being cooped up with Tyson in his underground sanctuary. The idea that anyone would find me here was ludicrous. *That was what I wanted though, right? I did not want anyone to stop me from my plan?* I was beginning to doubt my resolve, but at this point, I could not go anywhere even if I wanted to. Tyson had some how cut off my lines of communication with Evirent. No one knew where Tyson had gone once he left Joseph and Maria's, so I was going to have to see this through.

The thing that made it all worse was that I could not stop thinking about Jordan and how he was reacting to my letter. *Was he looking for me? Was he alright?* It was sheer misery being without him, and the anguish I was stewing in made Tyson all the more gleeful. Not only was he getting revenge on my father, he was also taking something precious away from me and Jordan in the process.

"Annaliessa, I was thinking if you give me a son, I will call him, Liam. Would that name be regal enough for a king?" I had no issue with the name, just the thought of bearing his son, and it was making me gag to have to think about it.

"What if you have a daughter? I have not heard you mention a girl's name once."

"I thought that name would be obvious. It will be Leah, of course, after her grandmother."

It was just too difficult to hold back the look of distress, and he clapped his hands and laughed with delight at my woe.

"We will need to head to what is left of your castle soon. We need to be on the same land where the curse originated in order to release it."

It was late evening by my mental calculations, and I knew it would take us a couple of hours to make the journey from here.

The time had arrived for us to depart and he had me wear my night dress. "Why would you insist on me wearing my night dress? It will be quite cool, as it is only early in the time of flowering. Surely you can do what you need to do to me in what I am wearing now." It was more of a statement than a question.

"I only have the privilege of bedding you once, and I want the benefit of the full experience."

I choked on my own bile and could not control the coughing fit that ensued.

His menacing look of rage was shaking me to the core. I was no longer sure he would honor any part of our agreement, but I was in no position to turn back now.

I did not enjoy the way he was scouring my body with his eyes, especially since the sheer fabric of this night dress shielded nothing from his smoldering gaze. I could see a bulge developing in his pants and it was all I could do to not scream. I am sure he would like that, and I was not going to give him any more satisfaction than what he was already enjoying in his mind.

Communication Breakthrough

32

We made the journey without being detected, and I watched him set up the instruments of his trade. It looked like he was ready to begin, but it seemed like he was hesitating and debating over something in his mind.

I suddenly felt lightness in my mind that had not been there the past couple of days, and I instantly heard Evirent in my thoughts.

"Where are you, Annaliessa? It is important that we find you. You do not have to go through with your plan. We have a way to give Tyson what he wants without you sacrificing yourself."

"What are you talking about, Evirent? Are you tricking me into giving up my location so you can stop what you know needs to happen. My father has to be brought to justice and we all need to be free."

"Your father has been brought to justice."

"What do you mean?"

"Your Father is in prison and will be executed once we have found you. That will satisfy Tyson's need for revenge."

"That may be, but it does not make us completely free."

"Do not be stubborn, Annaliessa. Now is not the time. Tell me where you are. I will eventually be able to detect it on my own, but I would rather you told me."

"I am at the place it all began."

"Do not go through with this, Annaliessa. I am on my way."

Hell's Fury

33

I saw a brilliant light flash in front of Tyson and him chant another spell that placed the curse of barrenness on my father. I felt something inside of me shift, like something being unlocked, and I knew the curse was lifted.

Tyson turned to me and I began to shiver violently. The look in his eyes was rotten to the core, and I knew I was in trouble, the hazardous kind of trouble, and there was going to be nothing gentle about this encounter.

"Take off your night dress, Annaliessa."

I could not move. My mind was reeling and my muscles were not responding.

He was removing his shirt, and as it dropped to the ground, I tried to turn and run, but it was ridiculous to think that I could out run magic.

My night dress was torn from my body by an invisible source. A tree root broke through the earth and ensnared my ankle, and I fell hard into the dirt, knocking the wind out of me. He was stripping away his pants, and I saw him fully erect and ready to take what I promised I would give him.

He came at me as if all the fury of hell was at his heels, and he pinned me to the ground as he laid himself on top of me. He bit my neck and I struggled underneath him. His grip tightened on my wrists which were held above my head. He brought his mouth down on my breast and lapped at my nipple. He then bit me hard enough to draw blood, and I bit down on my lip to keep from crying out. I did not want to give him the satisfaction of making me scream, but I was not sure if I was going to be victorious on that front.

He placed his hand on my breast next and began to twist it and squeeze it. I knew he was leaving his hand print bruised into my flesh, and I was powerless to stop him.

I felt another root come up from the ground and surround my wrists, so that he had free reign over my body to unleash his destructive vehemence. One hand was mangling my breast while the other found its desire between my legs. I felt his fingers slide into me, and Tyson moaned with pleasure or glee, I am not sure which. He was using his legs to keep mine spread open while he drove his fingers deeper into me. He was slamming his fist into my pelvic bone and it was starting to throb with pain. My lip was bleeding from where I was biting on it to keep from screaming.

He brought his face up to mine and licked the blood from my lip. It was sadistic, but was really just a distraction. His eyes were open and he wanted me looking at him so he could see my reaction to what he did next.

I felt burning hot pain shoot through my body as he plunged his hardness into me, way into me, and the scream came, and once it did I could not stop.

He rammed into me with such vigor that I could feel my back scraping against the ground and opening wounds that were going to be encrusted with dirt and stone. Each stroke was more painful than the last and I felt what must be blood dripping from my most tender and intimate place, and it seemed to be aiding him in his ability to come at me with more demanding thrusts. It felt as if I was being cut open and salt was being poured on the wound. I prayed it would stop soon. I will never forget the sound of delight that he emitted as he tore away my virtue. He was drunk with rage and I could hear him breathing hard from the exertion of his delirium. It seemed as if he was possessed, and I was the focus of his obsession. He was beginning to moan in a way that suggested he was finding this experience to be peaking in pleasure and I thought it must finally be about to end when he vacated me and I felt warm fluid dropping to my abdomen. I looked down to see his seed shooting from his device of torture onto me and once it had spent its load, it quickly retreated back into a limp appendage.

I was overwhelmed with horror at the fact that I had just endured being raped by this man, only to have him deny me the very thing I needed to produce a child.

"What have you done?!" I screamed at him. "Why, did you spew your seed on me rather than inside me, you demon of a man?!"

He was on his knees, but still between my legs. The evidence of what he had done to me was painted all over his crotch. My blood was everywhere, marking him with the cowardliness of his deed. He leaned over me and put his mouth by my ear, "Did you really think once was going to be enough? I plan on taking you as many times as I want before I finally plant my life inside you. I am going to enjoy this deal very much. Your soft warm sanctuary of muscle was a most rewarding experience, and I found the wave of pleasure it created was beyond anything I expected. You being so tense made it even more enjoyable than it would have been otherwise. I will not tire of that experience any time soon. My only regret is waiting for you to heal so I can take you again. Perhaps I should have thought that part out a bit and been somewhat gentler the first time."

I was feeling faint and sick. He stood up and grabbed my night dress that had been rent in two and wiped my blood from his body, and then he threw it at me.

The night sky was suddenly lit by fire, and it took me a moment to comprehend what I was seeing. The sky was full of at least two dozen dragons, and they seemed angry.

Tyson, still naked, began to chant and he managed to make some sort of shield around himself to protect him from the dragon's fiery wrath.

I was not protected and they realized that I would be in danger if they used this weapon while he was so close to me at this point in time.

I saw Jordan drop to the ground from one of the dragons and he came running toward me. I felt the roots release their hold and I scrambled to cover my naked and battered body from Jordan's view. The blood was rapidly spreading through the light fabric of what was left of my night dress. I was in rough shape, and it was going to be a long recovery, from the physical wounds. The other wounds, the ones to my mind and my soul, I was not convinced would ever heal.

Jordan was now at my side and he was crying uncontrollably. I could not console him, as I was bereft of feeling anything but pain and shame. He reached out his hand to touch my face, and I backed away from him. I was wrecked, and there was nothing he could do to fix it. I could not bear to disappoint him further, so retreating seemed the best option.

"Annaliessa, why, why did you feel you had to do this? I would have been happy with one child, with you, no one would have asked you to do this? You did not have to be the one to pay for another man's sins."

Jordan leaned in closer even though I tried to back away, and whispered, "He will pay for the damage he has done to you Annaliessa. I will make sure of it! Please do not leave me. Stay with me, my love."

"Annaliessa, please darling, stay with me. Did he finish the act? Did he leave you with child?"

I knew what he was asking, and I did not know what to say. I did not want to divulge my inability to gain that one consolation.

Tyson laughed sinisterly, and said, "No, I did not give her the distinction of bearing my child this time. Perhaps next time I lay with her she will be worthy enough to claim that prize."

The roar that came out of Jordan was gut-wrenching. I could tell that he wanted to rip Tyson limb from limb and feed him to the dogs.

"You will not have the chance to lay with her again!" Jordan spat out each word.

Tyson was working hard at maintaining the shield around him. I detected the strain in his voice at his last comment. The magic from the dragons must be building, and he will be vulnerable if they break through. I hoped they could break through, as I did not want to have to endure having this man look at me again, let alone touch me.

"What makes you think I will not claim what was promised to me?"

"I have something you want more."

"What do you think I could want more than fornicating with Annaliessa while you watch, completely helpless to stop me?"

Jordan ground his teeth, and stated plainly, "Her father."

"You want me to believe you can hand over her father?"

"I can and will. He is in prison right now awaiting death. You have the option of being his executioner if you wish, or you can simply just watch his head be separated from his neck if that would be satisfactory."

"Besides, any child you conceive outside of wedlock will not be a legitimate heir to the throne. A bastard child cannot rule. I think you have gotten far more than you bargained for. You have taken Annaliessa's virtue, and you can see her father die. I think you can release Annaliessa as having fulfilled her oath to you."

"Yes, I think you have a good point. I would enjoy seeing King Claude lose his head. Annaliessa is of little worth if she cannot give me a legitimate heir. Her remaining childless will be just as satisfying."

"What do you mean; her remaining childless?"

"What man is going to marry her and produce a legitimate heir? Oh, they might do it for the power that comes with the throne, but unless she has changed her mind about the man loving her and she returning that love, she will remain single the rest of her life."

"So I have your word? You will release her in exchange for her father?"

"Yes, please take her. She has given me the best part of herself; I have little use for anything else. I have your guarantee of protection."

"I have no plans to harm you," Jordan stated.

Tyson let down the shield, and instantly burst into flames. His screams filled the night air.

"I told you, I had no plans to harm you. I did not say anything about the dragons, however," Jordan said with satisfaction.

I was feeling so weak, and I knew I was losing consciousness from the blood loss and mental strain of the ordeal I had just been through. I fell back against the ground and Jordan quickly lifted me into his arms. The last thing I remember is him leaning down and placing a kiss on my forehead and the wetness of a tear was felt next to it.

"I love you, Annaliessa. That has not changed," was the whispered sentiment I vaguely recall hearing as I went under the blanket of reprieve, and the blackness that surrounded me was inviting me to stay.

Love's Plea

34

It was the young dragon, Seraphina, who had found a way to master her flame with precise accuracy that had snuck up to Tyson at an angle where Annaliessa would be safe, and killed him.

"I owe you a great deal of thanks, Seraphina, for ridding our land of that wicked warlock," said Jordan through his tears.

Seraphina nodded her head in acknowledgement and moved to Evirent's side. Her countenance was weighed down and not one of relief that one's enemy had been vanquished. She was a dusty-rose colored dragon with a brownish-red feathering, similar in appearance to clay. She was half the size of Evirent, but just as deadly when the occasion called for it.

"Evirent, my father told me the story about how you saved my life before I was even born. Can you do the same for Annaliessa now? She is losing a great deal of blood and I am starting to fear that she will not live long without your aid."

"Jordan what you ask will only heal her physical wounds not the deep wounds to her emotions, mind and spirit. She may never heal from these. Do you understand this?"

"Yes, I understand, but I would rather have her alive and next to me, than dead and buried where I cannot touch her or look upon her."

"You are too young to know the devastation that this deed leaves in its wake. She may be alive, but she may not ever be reachable if her mind has drifted to a plane beyond the one we exist in. You will see her, but you will never hold her or converse with her if she remains in this state. Do you think you can bear watching her breathe, yet not really being present with you? It would be worse than her death. You would be staring at a reminder of what you will never have, and be unable to free yourself to move on. You have a kingly destiny you need to fulfill, and you will need a wife to complete it. Will you be able to turn your back on her and do what is necessary if her mind is lost forever?"

"I fully comprehend what you are telling me, and I will cross that bridge when I get to it. Annaliessa is strong, and I know she will come back to me eventually. I cannot risk letting her die. It is worth the price; she is worth the price!"

"Very well, I will give you what you ask. Tell everyone to leave the area, as this is not something we want to share openly."

"I am ordering all the armies and everyone other than myself and the dragons to leave the area and do not look back. I will see to Annaliessa's safe return to my home, and to her physical care."

The other princes were hesitant to leave with the armies, and hung back at the scene of the crime.

"What are you waiting for? Why are you not leaving with the others?" Jordan shouted at them.

"You are not the only one concerned for Annaliessa's health and well-being. Have you forgotten, that only a couple of moon cycle's ago, we were all tied to her. We all owe her a debt that we can never repay, and we are not leaving," said Prince Kalvin.

"Evirent reached out to the princes' minds and spoke calmly, but commandingly, to them. *"If you want her to live, you will do what Prince Jordan asked you to do."*

"Why are we not privy to what you are about to do? Why is only Prince Jordan able to see what is going to take place?" asked Prince Josiah.

"Should there be a time when you need to have this knowledge; it will be shared with you. Now is not that time. You are dismissed. Please leave now, before my patience wears thinner," Evirent said in a silent commanding voice to each one's mind.

The princes reluctantly collected their belongings and turned to join the retreating armies.

Once they were a good distance off, the dragons surrounded me and Annaliessa in a circle to close off any prying eyes from the gifting that was about to occur.

Seraphina asked if she could be the one to share the gift of healing with Annaliessa. Evirent looked proud of his young daughter and acquiesced to her offer.

"Jordan, do you have a vessel that will collect my blood?" Seraphina queried.

"Yes, I have a wooden bowl in my pack. Let me get it for you."

"What would you like me to do?" Jordan asked.

"I am going to lift a scale from my leg, and you need to prick it lightly with your knife. You need to hold the bowl up to the area and collect a cupful of blood. Once you have it, move aside so I can seal the wound with my saliva."

"You must get her to awaken so that she can drink the blood. She may resist, but it is important that she drinks it all."

"I will do as you say," I said plainly.

Seraphina raised the scale over the vein in her leg at a spot where I would be able to reach easily. I drew my knife, and placed the bowl to the spot with my other hand. I quickly pricked the vein, and watched as her magical infused blood sprinkled into the bowl.

"That is enough," she said to my mind.

I stepped back and she brought her head down and licked the wound. The blood stopped flowing immediately, and she placed the scale back down where it belonged.

I lifted Annaliessa up to a sitting position, with her resting against my chest. "Annaliessa," I called to her, trying to pull her back to me. She was unresponsive. I could feel the blood from her wounds on her back seeping into my shirt. I was shaking from the emotion that was racking my mind and body, and it was sucking the strength from my very bones. If she did not awaken soon, I was sure I was going to collapse from the exhaustion of the ordeal.

I put my lips to her ear and kissed her lightly, and then I called her name once again. I felt her stir, and her eyes fluttered open slightly. "Annaliessa, I have medicine for you to drink that will heal you. Please, darling, you must drink it."

She looked like she was fighting to remain conscious. She was so weak and frail it scared me. I could see she was trying to form words, but her body was not cooperating. She was still trying to resist my help, but this time I was not going to let her push me away.

I managed to get the bowl to her lips and get her to drink it. She reacted the way I expected from the taste, and she almost did not keep it down. It only took a few seconds, but I could feel her body relaxing again. She was still in a semi-conscious state and all I wanted to do now was get her home to Vulterrian. That is where she belonged, and I was going to make sure she stayed there this time.

I carried her to Evirent, and with some help from Seraphina, we mounted him for the ride home. She was safe in my arms once again, and I prayed she would heal completely from all the wounds that monster had inflicted on her.

We were airborn in seconds and she slipped back into the blackness of an unconscious slumber. *Do not worry, my princess, everything will work out. It has too,* was the only thought in my head.

Justice Rendered

35

It had been seven days since the rape had occurred, and while my body had healed remarkably fast thanks to the intervention of the dragons, my mind was still a fractured mess. The nightmares were unbelievably vivid, and I relived the pain every time I drifted to sleep. Needless to say, I was avoiding sleep like it was a disease. In fact, it was in a way, a blight to my soul. I felt numb, and Jordan was finding the sharp side of my tongue could wield a pretty deep cut. I did not want to hurt him, but he would not leave me alone. I know that in time he will see it is better for him this way, but it stills feels foreign to push him away. Why he does not take the hint to leave me alone? I do not understand. The thought of any man touching me right now sends violent shivers through my body, and chokes off my ability to breathe. It gets so bad that I end up vomiting every time. *Is that what he really wants; a wife who is afraid to have him touch her, and if he gets too close she'll heave her stomach contents onto him? Why is he being so hard-headed?*

I tried to push these thoughts aside, as today was the day that my father's execution was to be carried out. I should be relieved or happy that he is finally going to pay for all the horrible things he has done, or allowed to happen, but I cannot feel anything; my soul is vacant. I do not even want to attend the event, but my presence is required. The people are demanding retribution for my suffering.

I would rather stay in my assigned room at the Vulterrian castle. I really want to go home, but Jordan is insisting that I live here where he can look after me. I think it is more like he wants to ensure that I do not do anything else rash or risky. Evirent will not even answer my pleas. His ears have gone deaf to my cries.

I am dragged out of bed by a half dozen servants to get me presentable for the festivities. People are carrying on like it is some big party when in fact it should be a somber occasion. I am feeling nauseous, and my head is starting to pound. *I hope no one expects me to make any kind of speech. I have nothing to say at this point.*

I am escorted down to an awaiting carriage a couple of hours later, and Jordan is there to help me enter it. He offers his hand for me to use for stability in climbing in, but I refuse to take it. My mother is already inside the carriage and she reaches out her hand to me. I take it and grab the door of the carriage and hoist myself up and in. Jordan follows quickly behind with a frown on his face.

My mother looks at me with sad eyes. She understands the suffering I am going through, to some degree. After all, my father was never kind to her when he claimed his marital rights, but at least he did not despise her to the core when he did it. He did not leave her to die, as Tyson had left me. *I am not certain. Would it have felt differently if it were my husband attacking me, or would it have been worse? I think, perhaps, I have done my mother a disservice in assuming what she endured was less dreadful than mine. I only had to face revulsion once. She had to endure the treachery of a wicked, deranged man for over seventeen years.*

My mother looked younger than she had even a short time ago. She seemed to carry herself more regally, and had a smile on her face, except when with me. With me she was more like her old self, sad and withdrawn. *Was it really that easy to let the past go and move on as she was making it seem?* I must learn her secret, because I was drowning in my sorrow and shame, and it was beginning to pull me under.

We arrived at the execution location. My father was sentenced to be beheaded with his own sword. Jordan's father, King Nicholas, was the one selected by lot to perform the execution.

Jordan disembarked the carriage, and assisted my mother in her extrication. He motioned to me to come forward, but I shook my head. "I will watch from here. I really do not want to be on display and have to see everyone's look of pity." I diverted my glance away from him, so I would not have to see the look of disapproval cross his brow. The carriage door closed and Jordan escorted my mother to her seat in the stands that had been built for the royals.

All the kings and queens, as well as the princes were here. Wait, I did not see Samuel. *What could be the reason he was excused from these festivities, and yet I was forced to come?*

I heard a rap on the carriage door. I peered out and saw Samuel standing there. "Is there something I can help you with, Samuel?"

"I want to talk to you, if that would be permitted."

"You can talk, as long as you do not anticipate that I will respond."

"Thank-you, Annaliessa, for extending me this privilege." With that he opened the carriage door and climbed in. Jordan had not noticed, or he would be here in a heartbeat.

"Annaliessa, as you know I am rather shy. This took all my nerve to come over here to talk to you, so I hope you will listen to what I have to say."

I did not move or indicate that I would be willing to do anything. I guess he took that as permission to continue, because he pressed on with what he had to say.

"The hardest thing I have had to do these past few moon cycles has been to entertain young women with whom I am to choose a bride. I had never really considered having to do this. For some, I suppose, it is a rather fun and fruitful experience, but it has been tedious for me. I always felt relieved that I would not have to endure the courtship rituals the way most must, as I was bound to you

144

until a short time ago. Maybe it was because we had grown up together that I felt comfortable around you, or maybe it was just the bonding. I just want you to know that it has come to my relief that I am able to marry anyone at this point, all thanks to you and your sacrifice. I would like to marry for love, but given my lack of ease in conversing with women, I am leaning toward an arranged marriage."

"I guess what I am trying to say to you is that, sometimes things do not work out the way we had planned or anticipated, and while at first it seems difficult to deal with, if we work through it and change the way we look at the situation, we can find peace and resolution to the things that distress us. The things that make us afraid no longer seem so scary. We can entertain something that most likely will be better in the end than what we would have had if we were never expected to do anything differently at all. Does that make sense to you?"

I stared at him, and wondered when he had become so mature. He was a shy young man, and that made him appear more boyish than the other princes, but the person sitting across from me now was no longer a boy. I expected him to look away, but he did not concede. He was not going to let me remain silent.

"Samuel, I know the courage and determination it must have taken for you to share this with me. I will think upon it, I promise."

He was satisfied with my answer and rose to leave the carriage. I shocked myself by grabbing his arm before he descended. "Samuel, wait."

He looked back at me just as stunned. "What is it, Annaliessa?"

"I know it is hard for you to express your feelings and to be comfortable with others, especially women, but do not give up on finding love. Do not agree to marry someone just because it is convenient and will save you some embarrassment. You deserve more than that. Do not settle for less. Promise me, Samuel. I did not endure the humiliating shame of rape, for you to compromise. Find love, Samuel. Promise me you will."

"How can I deny you that request, Annaliessa? How could any of us deny you that? You are right. I will put aside my unease and discomfort, just as you did for me. That is the least I can do to show you my gratitude."

"Annaliessa, when I find her; you will be one of the first to know." A tear ran down his cheek, and he quickly retreated.

The hour was at hand. My father was brought to the stage and forced to kneel and lay his head upon the wooden block. The charges were read and King Nicholas stepped up to him and unsheathed the sword. I hung my head and cried as the sound of the sword slicing through bone and connecting with wood rang out. A triumphant shout went up through the crowd as my father's life drained out onto the floor. I only felt remorse that it happened too late to change my fate.

Aftermath

36

Jordan could not understand why the death of my father did not bring me around. He had anticipated that I would be able to pull myself out of this depression afterward, and was disheartened that I remained withdrawn.

I had been relocated to my old bedroom at the Vulterrian castle, the one that was connected to the secret passage, after I refused to attend Prince Charles' seventeenth birthday during the sun's zenith. I was surprised Queen Sarah did not object, but these days, leniency was being encouraged where I was concerned.

My own birthday was just over a moon cycle away. I was still not talking much, and hibernated in my room mostly. Jordan would insist on taking me out to the garden at least once every day for a couple of hours. I did not mind this time, as we sat quietly by the pond and fed the fowl that gathered there. I was actually beginning to look forward to the excursion now, and I found it peaceful. I felt like something inside my heart was being mended there as I marveled at the intricacies of nature. There was beauty all around me, and this was my favorite season, so I felt the cloud of darkness I had been enshrouded in lift a bit more each day.

I did not know how he could remain so dedicated and patient. I wanted him to be happy, and I knew I could not give him this basic necessity, and yet he seemed content to wait. It upset me that he was denying himself the opportunity to find happiness with another woman, and I finally burst and dumped my frustration out on him.

"Jordan, why do you insist on being here with me every day? You have even learned it is better if you say nothing and remain silent, and yet you still do it. Why not spend this time with another young woman who will entertain your intellect and possibly acquire your heart? Did I not make it possible for you to have all that? Why do you disregard my gift and mock me?"

I saw him clamp his jaw tight. He was forcing himself to not say the angry retort that was on the tip of his tongue.

"Annaliessa, I am with the woman who entertains my intellect, even when she is silent. You are the woman who captured my heart, and I have no intention of taking it back. I gave it to you freely, and it is yours to do with as you please. I recognize that one day you will forgive yourself and the others that hurt you, like your father and Tyson. When you experience the release of that forgiveness, I will be here, ready and waiting, to welcome you into my arms forever. Nothing has changed for me, Annaliessa. I want you to be my wife now and forever. I love you, I always have, and I always will."

"You want me, a used, lifeless shell of a being? Really, Jordan, you do not have to be polite on my account. You have done your duty, and no one would fault you for moving on."

"I do not know how to make you believe that I love you. I do not care that you no longer have your maiden's virtue, Annaliessa. He may have had that one night, but I am the one you will spend the rest of your days with. My longing for our wedding night has not waned. It will still be beautiful and full of meaning, uniting our souls together as one. It will not be like your nightmares. I want to eradicate those from your memory with my love, Annaliessa, but I cannot do that without your consent and cooperation. Any tie you had to Tyson, died with him that night."

"Do you know why the dragon's saved you, Annaliessa?"

I shook my head no.

"They told me that you were always meant for me. Because I had the blood of a dragon flowing through me, I would be drawn to someone who was pure of heart. You proved to be more than anything they had expected, and that is why they saved you. You, too, have this blood flowing through you, and if you stop focusing on your pain, you will feel the pull of it, and it will lead you straight to me. If you do not believe me and what I say to you, then believe it, as that blood cannot lie; it always seeks truth and purity."

I could not deny what he was saying. I had felt the pull toward him when we were in this place. Perhaps that was the very essence of why I felt better just being silent here with him every day. I also understood what he said about giving me his heart. I originally had this same sentiment toward Tyson. Until I found that his heart was wicked and sinister deep down. I knew this was not the case with Jordan, as the blood coursing through my veins would have declared otherwise. *He was good, far too good to end up with me, right?* was the question ringing through my mind.

Birthday Extravaganza

37

It seems impossible that I am on the brink of turning twenty. At least my mother rescinded the requirement for me to marry in just over a year. No one argued the point; given what I had been through, they knew it would take time, and lots of it.

Unlike other birthday celebrations, I could not escape mine. My mother insisted on it, and Jordan was all too happy to comply. The party was to be held in the central kingdom of Heraldin, to make it easy for everyone from all the kingdoms to attend. This was to be my big public coming out event for the first time since the tragic night of my disgrace.

We arrived the day before the party, and while Prince Kalvin had hoped to spend some personal time with me before the party (I think mostly out of courtesy, and not desire) Jordan was not allowing it. He did not want me upset by anything. *Who had assigned him my guardian or keeper? I was not sure, but he was taking the job very seriously.* I really did not mind. I did not want to talk to anyone, so it was better this way. I had barely started to converse with Jordan in more pleasant terms, and I was not up to having to maintain any kind of appearances before the big party. That was going to be excruciating enough.

The gown my mother had commissioned for the occasion was exceptionally beautiful. It was a cream color, since white made me look pale. It had emerald beading on the bodice and an intricate, green stitched pattern on the skirt. It looked like water lilies, or maybe that was just my impression, as I had spent so much time at the pond over the past couple of moon cycles, that I had them on my mind. I smiled at the thought of the pond, and noticed that the emptiness I had initially felt after the incident was not as vast anymore. I was smiling. *What had come over me?* I was actually missing the time with Jordan at the pond and thinking about the time fondly. Perhaps something was about to change in my life, beside my age.

My hair was pulled up, and long tendrils of curls were left dangling around my face and neck. I had a simple tiara with emeralds and diamonds to adorn my head, and a single emerald on a gold chain around my neck. My makeup was simple, but it put color onto my face and made the shallow-yellowed hallows in my cheeks that had appeared recently, recede. I looked healthy and normal, and I found it was encouraging to see myself this way. I was not sure I would ever feel normal again, but tonight I at least looked like I was, and it felt good; surprisingly good, in fact.

It was an evening ball, so dinner was just with the royal families. My mother thought this was best so I would not tire too easily. Everyone was seated at the table when I arrived in the dining hall. The spot next to Jordan was vacant, and he stood as soon as he saw me enter the room.

Everyone turned to stare in my direction, and the look of adoration on Jordan's face made me start to warm inside. Everyone complimented me on how beautiful I looked, and I took my seat next to Jordan. I was finally allowed to sit next to him at a dining table, and it made me relax. He would not push me to talk, and I felt my spirits lighten, and it spread to my countenance without me even realizing it.

"You are smiling. What has you in such a glorious mood this evening?"

"Hmm." I was not aware I was smiling. "I guess I am relaxed that I can eat in silence and not have to entertain any bantering of conversation, since you understand how difficult it is for me to discuss trivial matters right now."

"I will take that as a compliment," Jordan said. "Annaliessa, you look stunning tonight. You will have to forgive me if I keep staring at you. I am finding it difficult to focus on anything else but you right now."

A blush actually crept up my cheeks, and I pretended to be extremely interested in my place setting. *Why did this compliment have me responding like this, and now of all times?* Something was definitely happening inside me, and I was not sure whether to fight it, or let it have its way. I was leaning toward letting it have its way.

After dinner, we took our places at the entrance hall to welcome the arriving guests. It was awkward to be the focus of so much attention, but it comes with the territory of being a princess.

I was greeting a young woman when I sensed Jordan tense up. I looked up to see what could be the source of his distress, and saw Alexander approaching. *Was he still jealous of Alexander? That was silly, especially given how I have barely given Jordan any notice as of late. Why would he think I would give another man any?*

"Alexander, how nice of you to come," I said politely. "I would like to introduce you to my mother, Queen Amanda."

"Mother, this is Alexander from Marcynth. He trades with the far northern kingdoms, and I am sure he has plenty of interesting tales to tell about his travels there. Is that not correct, Alexander?"

"Yes, Princess Annaliessa, I have enough tales to fill an entire evening to be sure."

"It is a pleasure to meet you, Alexander, and to find that a sense of adventure is alive and well in our land. I trust the journey you take to these kingdoms is safe from harm."

"Most of the time it is. There are occasions where it can be risky, but then I travel with a small band of armed men to ensure these risks are mitigated in my favor. If you will permit me Your Majesty, I would like to share a few insights with you on the dance floor this evening, assuming I am not overstepping my boundaries in asking."

"I am sure our dancing together would raise more than a few eyebrows this evening. Perhaps a more formal meeting can be arranged tomorrow, and you can share the information you desire."

"I will await your invitation, Your Majesty."

"How about you, Princess Annaliessa? Is your dance card open or closed to only one person this evening?" he said, giving Jordan a snide glance.

"I am afraid that I have not quite regained all my strength back yet, Alexander, so the few dances I will engage in this evening, will be reserved for the princes."

"It is good to see you out in public and enjoying yourself; and that will be enough to satisfy me," Alexander said with a demure smile. He bowed and moved off into the ballroom.

The night went by quickly, and I found it was not as awful as I had anticipated. It was nice to interact with and talk to the princes again, and they were so kind and generous to amuse me. Most of the guests, outside of the royal families and nobility, had already gone. I was exhausted and excused myself just before the second watch of the night. This was the hardest watch as it was the darkest and most prone to attacks and treachery.

I entered my room, and flung myself onto the bed. I was about to drift asleep when I heard a knock at the door. I knew who it was, and though I was tired, I found I did not want to tell him to go away.

"Jordan, you can come in. I am still dressed."

The door opened and he seemed to glide across the floor to the bed. He plopped himself down on the bed next to me so that we were lying side by side.

"Did you have fun tonight, Annaliessa?"

"Actually, I did. Are you surprised?"

"A little, but something was different about you tonight. You seemed more like the woman I had known earlier this year; the one I had known all my life."

"Truth be told, I felt more like her tonight than I had before."

He turned onto his side so that he was looking at me. "Annaliessa, do you think it would be alright if I kissed you goodnight?"

I felt a twinge of panic rise, but pushed it back down. I knew I had nothing to fear with Jordan, and I was curious if I would be able to engage in any form of intimacy again. Who better to test this with than the one person I trusted with my life? He was the one person I would always love.

"Yes, Jordan, you can kiss me goodnight." My heart began to quicken its tempo, and my palms began to sweat, but not out of fear; out of anticipation.

He leaned over and took my cheek in his hand, brushing light circles on it with his thumb. "I love you," he said as he bent his head to my lips. The kiss was sweet and gentle, not forceful or demanding in any way. He did not press me for entrance with his tongue. He was scared and hopeful at the same time.

When he pulled away and started to rise from the bed, I whispered, "Thank-you."

"*Thank-you* for what, Annaliessa?"

"For patiently loving me even when I have made it onerous, and for being the kind and considerate man that you are, not demanding what I cannot give you yet."

"I will wait as long as I have to, Annaliessa. I told you, I am not going anywhere. You are the one I want to be with, forever and always."

He left my room and I fell asleep instantly where I lay. It was the first night I had slept without a nightmare, and if his kisses were the cure to eradicating those permanently, I was going to let him kiss me as often as he liked.

Northern Potential

38

I was to find out later, that while I blissfully slept in, plans were being put into motion that would perhaps change the landscape of our land for centuries to come.

¥

"Alexander, welcome. Please come sit and have a cup of tea," said Queen Amanda, with warmth that was hard to say no to.

"Thank-you for allowing me this audience with you, Your Majesty."

"You have a proposal to share with me that would benefit not only my kingdom, but perhaps our entire land, and I am anxious to hear it, so please do not delay any further in sharing it."

"I have been travelling to the kingdom of Icelandica, in the far north, since I was a young boy of thirteen. I travelled with my father, as he wanted me to experience as much of life as possible, and saw these expeditions as a way of expanding our influence outside the borders of our land. I have gotten to know the king and his children very well over the years. In fact, just two years ago, the king lost his beloved wife. He has several wives, in fact, but the others were taken to form agreements with other kingdoms in the north. This wife was the wife of his youth, and he loved her deeply. I think he is at the point where he could open his heart to another once again, and you might be the kind of woman that could capture it."

"You are suggesting that I marry this king? What is his name?"

"Phillipe is his name, and yes, that is what I am implying could be possible."

"What would my marrying King Phillipe, outside of love, of course, mean to our land and to my kingdom?"

"His land is rich in precious gems, coal and iron. Things we need to maintain our strength, and to trade to other lands, and perhaps across the ocean."

"Alexander, your quest for expansion is quite grandiose. While I am not opposed to marrying again, this time I will only do it for love. I have endured the rigors of life without it, and will not enslave myself to it ever again."

"I am willing to entertain an expedition to meet this king, but I will not make any promises beyond that. When are you suggesting we leave for this visit?"

"Given that the snowy season is almost upon us, and it is a two moon cycle journey, I recommend we leave at the time of the tree budding. Would that arrangement be suitable, Your Majesty?"

"Yes, I think that is a possibility, provided I do not have a wedding to plan."

"You think Prince Jordan and Princess Annaliessa will actually marry?"

"My dear boy, you do not understand the power of love. Once you have experienced it, you will know why I believe without a doubt that the two of them will wed. I think it will be sooner, rather than later at that."

"Prince Jordan is a very lucky man, Your Majesty."

"I would have to say that it is my daughter who is most blessed. They will make each other very happy, and this is my greatest wish."

"We will talk again after the turn of the year, and make the necessary plans."

"Thank-you again, and I look forward to our next meeting, Your Majesty."

I wonder what this King Phillipe is really like? Could I really be so fortunate as to find love at this point in my life? I should not get my hopes up, but it is intriguing to consider. These thoughts are dangerous to consider, Queen Amanda reminded herself. Perhaps I am getting the cart before the horse.

Wedding Surprise

39

I heard a knock on my bedroom door, and thought it must be Jordan. Who else would disturb me? I had fallen asleep in my dress, so I made my way to the door, groggy, but full of anticipation. I was glad I did not have to wait to make myself presentable, as I was excited to tell him that I slept without the nightmare.

I was stunned when I saw Prince Samuel outside the door. He smiled sheepishly, and apologized for waking me.

"It is alright, Samuel, I do not usually sleep this late, or this much, so how could you have known you would be waking me since it is almost lunchtime, as you pointed out."

"Annaliessa, I have something very important I need to share with you right away, as my family will be leaving for home in the next hour. Would you be able to meet me in the solarium in twenty minutes?"

"Sure, Samuel, just let me change into something less formal, and I will be right down."

Samuel seemed nervous, and this was totally out of character for him to request to see me so urgently. I was a bit worried about the news he had for me, as the last meeting of its kind led me down a rather difficult path. I hurriedly changed, removed my jewelry and tiara, leaving my hair up, and a bit disheveled.

The solarium here in the Heraldin castle was gorgeous. It was like the sun's zenith time all year-round. The leaded glass doors that led into this sanctuary of living color sparkled with the light streaming in from the glass dome canopy above. During the snowy moon cycles, they lit the fireplaces that were built-in to the outer stone portion of the wall to keep everything alive and make it comfortable for human visitation. The fireplaces vented directly to the outside, leaving the space toasty and inviting. There was a wooden bridge over a large pond that surrounded and separated a smaller piece of land, making it like an island in the center. There was a large beech tree that grew in the middle of that island, and that is where Samuel was waiting.

He stood when he saw me approach, and the smile that split his face relaxed me. No one could smile like that and bear bad news.

"Annaliessa, just as I promised, I wanted you to be one of the first to know. Outside of our parents, it has not been made official yet, I made them promise I would get to tell you first," he gushed out rapidly.

"Samuel, slow down. Tell me what?"

"I fell in love, Annaliessa, and I am getting married just before the trees bud, on my birthday."

It took me a few seconds to process what he just said, and then our conversation the day of my father's execution rang through my head. "Samuel, that is wonderful! Who is she?"

"She is the daughter of the captain of our personal guard. Her name is Sharon. I asked her to marry me before we left to attend your party, and she said yes!" He was practically jumping up and down he was so excited.

"How did you two meet and begin your courtship?"

"My father, the captain, and I were discussing some business and missed our dinner. In walks this lovely girl with inviting olive skin, chocolate brown hair, and eyes that made me forget my own name. I think my mother may have planned this little event, but I am so happy that it happened. I asked the captain the next day if I could spend an hour with his daughter, and the rest is history. I was in love by the end of that hour, and saw her every day for two moon cycles."

"Annaliessa, I cannot thank you enough for making me promise to try for love. If you had not, I hate to think of what my life would be without it. Now that I have experienced it, I would perish if I were to lose it. Your selfless display of love and honor had a profound effect on me, and if I were to guess, on us all."

"Oh, Samuel, you have given me such hope! If you are the only one that finds love, I can live knowing that I made a difference in someone's life, and it is like a sweet salve to my soul." The tears were in my eyes, and I was not ashamed to let him see them.

I felt validation for all the evil I endured, with the smile on his face. In that moment, I was grateful that the past events set in motion the happiness of this young man and his betrothed. Yes, unconditional love can change things; it can change things a great deal if we allow it to. The key was in not only giving it, but feeling worthy to receive it in return, and I felt something deep within begin to draw from his exuberance, like a light was breaking through darkness. I desperately wanted to see Jordan, and he was my next priority.

Samuel and I said our farewells, but I stayed by the tree. I was feeling so peaceful, I could not bear to leave quickly, but wanted to stay and take in the moment just a little longer.

Climbing Trees

40

I saw Samuel outside her door as I was coming around the corridor. He was asking to meet her in the solarium. The familiar pangs of jealousy started to rise up and grip my heart, and I had to concentrate on breathing slowly to keep it under control.

I waited until she went down to the solarium and followed a few seconds behind her. I was going to follow her in and eavesdrop on their conversation to ensure that his intentions were pure, as the last time I left her alone, something terrible happened. I was scared, and I was not above admitting it to myself. I do not think I could survive another ordeal like the last one. I barely managed to hang on to her then, and our relationship is tentative at this point. I cannot do anything to scare her away, but between the fear and the jealousy, I was like a caged animal ready to attack anyone or anything that got close.

I realized that if I could not trust Annaliessa with Samuel, then our relationship was like a house of wooden blocks, the kind children play with. One wrong move and it tumbles down. I had to trust her, regardless of the irrational feelings that were enslaving me. If I failed this test, then I had no business pursuing Annaliessa in any kind of a relationship.

I decided to wait on the bench across the hall from the solarium so I could see when Samuel or Annaliessa left. I waited, impatiently, mind you. I chewed on my fingernails and bit one down so far that I actually drew blood. *I could not keep this up. How would I explain my bandaged fingers to her?* I again focused on breathing rhythmically, and remembered the small kiss I shared with her last night. Before yesterday, I was beginning to lose faith that things would work out for Annaliessa and me. I had always believed that love would conquer the evil that had tried to destroy our lives; that it was the most powerful force in our land, but she was making me doubt my beliefs. She was making me doubt everything I believed.

It seemed interminably long, but Samuel finally left. Annaliessa had not followed him out, so I pounced on the opportunity to find her alone and perhaps remind her of love's power to conquer all.

I saw her sitting under the tree in the middle of the solarium. She looked really happy even though she had tears falling from her eyes.

I cleared my throat and asked, "Annaliessa, is everything alright?"

"Jordan, everything is as it should be. Samuel is getting married, and he is in love. He is in love, Jordan, can you believe it? He is marrying for love and not obligation, and I could not be more ecstatic!"

I breathed a sigh of relief and closed the distance between us with a few long strides. She rose to her feet and leapt into my arms as I reached her. Her hug was genuine, and I felt a strength to it that I had not felt for far too long. She was coming back to me. She had to be. There was no other explanation. I knew what to do to ensure she would return to me.

"What do you say we climb this tree to celebrate your new found joy?"

She laughed authentically, and it was like the sound of angels singing, or at least what I imagined they would sound like. "You first, or shall I show you how it is done?"

"Are you challenging me, Annaliessa? You know you have no chance of winning, right?"

She did not even give me a retort, but jumped and grabbed the first branch. She was at a distinct disadvantage in her dress, and I was not going to give her an opportunity to best me. No, I was going to be waiting for her in the middle of that tree, so that I could take her safely into my arms and remind her how much we belonged together.

She had gotten herself draped over the first branch, and I easily swung myself up and over it and was onto the next. She was glowing she was so happy, and she was chiding me that I had an unfair advantage since I was not in a dress.

I got myself up to the third branch and leaned over it to help her up to the second. I assisted her up to my branch and held her to me. I never want this moment to end. I felt so alive with her in my arms, and with her so happy, it was like nothing had happened. It was as if all those horrible time had been erased.

"Jordan, perhaps we can sit here on the branch like we did in your tree when we were kids?"

"I was hoping you would say that." The emotions flooding me were so overpowering. *Was she feeling as giddy as I was?* I felt like that little boy again; excited, scared, and full of anticipation.

It was a beautiful silence where we shared a communion of fellowship with each other that words can never satisfy. I hope she felt my acceptance and the assurance that she belonged in my arms. She was the very air I breathed, and it was rich with a splendid aroma that tickled my senses, and awakened my curiosity. I wanted to be her banner of protection, where she would always feel at home, safe, and secure, and would never think of leaving again.

Wooing

41

The turning of the leaves was in the last stages now that the snowy season was just a moon cycle away. Jordan was turning nineteen today, and had specifically requested no party. He only wanted to spend it with his family and with me. I felt privileged to be included in his family. The past two moon cycles had been magnificent. We had grown close again, and our friendship had mended and fused us together like two peas in a pod.

That day we spent in the tree at the Heraldin solarium was a turning point for me. It was like my soul had been tightly wrapped in upon itself, like a rosebud before it blooms. I could feel the petals unfurling and opening to receive the warmth from the sun in my soul, and Jordan was the sun. I knew then that I could not picture being anywhere but under his gaze.

I had been walking so long in the desert, the sun had felt burdensome and oppressive, but I had discovered that day that he, in fact, was my oasis. The place in the desert where the stream flowed and gave life to the succulent blossoms that drew from its essence, and I was actually blooming under his attentive care. I needed the sun and the stream, and he was the source behind both. His love was indeed powering the energy I felt surging inside of me, and breaking down barriers I had established to protect myself from the perceived threat of disappointing him further. I know my actions shattered him, and it had to have been difficult for him to come to terms with the loss of what should have been his wholly and unreservedly, but he never once made it seem like it was of any real consequence. I do not know why I had not realized before that the only thing he ever cared about losing was me.

I also knew he wanted us to be more than friends, but I was still struggling with the issue of intimacy. I was frightened to open this avenue of exploration, and he was being very patient in waiting for me to join him at the summit of what was to be the culmination of our love. I wanted to be with him. I just did not want to hurt again.

I was assured by my mother and his, that the pain of my first experience would not be repeated in any manner. I would most certainly enjoy this foray into sexual enlightenment with an intensity I would find hard to squelch, given our strong feelings and commitment to each other.

I am sure I was erring on the cautious side, but I did not want to venture down a path I would need to retreat from if I was not completely sure it was the right one or the right time.

I knew Jordan was struggling to not demand more in this area of our relationship than I was willing to give, and it was taking a toll on him. Our kisses were getting more passionate as of late, and it was stirring things in him that were best left alone if I was not ready to take our relationship to the point of marriage. He was still being the gallant man of integrity, but his resolve was weakening. Truth be told, my resolve was diminishing as well. We were both like the forest during the sun's zenith after no rain, tinder dry and ready to ignite.

We had a lovely dinner with his family, and had spent a wonderful evening engaging in discussions about all sorts of fancy. It was drawing late and Jordan announced that he was going to retire for the evening. I excused myself as well, and he walked me to my room.

"Annaliessa, I want to take you to the beach tonight. Would you be willing to join me?"

"Jordan, I know the watchful eye of your parents has been lifted to some extent, but do you not think that might be a bit risky? I am sure they have noticed that I am not as aloof as I had been previously, and they must be getting a bit more anxious about where our relationship is heading. Do you not think that tonight of all nights, they might actually check to ensure we are not alone together, as had been our custom earlier this year?"

"I will deal with the consequences if that is the case. I have set up something special, and I want to share it with you."

"Alright, when should I be ready for you?"

"I will come for you in an hour or so. I think my parents seemed quite enraptured with each other tonight, and I am sure they will be retiring shortly themselves."

I blushed at what he was implying. *After all,* I thought, *they are married. Why would they not enjoy the fruits of that union? It is perfectly natural. It is me who is unable to see it as healthy and beneficial, well at least it has been.*

Being around Jordan's parents made me realize that what I had experienced was far from normal, and that what should transpire between a man and his wife was a splendid and beautiful thing. I wanted that, I was just uncertain as to how much, but I had a feeling I would soon find out.

He kissed me on the cheek quickly and sprinted to his room.

Passion Ignited

42

I heard the familiar knock on the passageway panel, and raced to answer it. I had changed into a less formal but warm gown, had a coat and had shoes on my feet. I had also grabbed a couple of blankets, just in case.

Jordan looked incredibly alluring tonight. He was bundled for the cold and had a couple of blankets in his arms as well. He was quiet, nodded in acceptance of what I had on, and turned to lead the way down the corridor.

He was a bit edgy, but not in a distressing sense. I was a little intrigued by his silence. I tried to press him for what this special arrangement was, but he let my inquisition bounce right off of him. He was maintaining his silence, and nothing was going to rid him of his secret until it was time to be unveiled.

It was a calm night. The wind was not blowing like the last time we made this journey, which was a good thing, since it was cold enough already.

I felt the sand begin to work its way inside my shoe, and it was cold and gritty, yet spoke of adventure and lured me on to capture my prize.

He had blocked the entrance to the alcove area with potted reeds. I am sure this was to help block any wind as well as provide privacy. He stopped abruptly in front of me and told me to close my eyes. He really was taking this to the extreme. I obliged, and he led me inside the alcove.

He took the blankets from my arms, and I could feel a heat source nearby. He took my coat and removed my shoes, and all the while I was not allowed to even peek a little bit.

I felt him stand behind me and wrap his arms around me, and he whispered in my ear, "Open your eyes."

It was stunning really. A fire burned brightly, warming the place, and oil lamps were lit all over the enclosed space. The light flickered off the walls providing an intricate show with the skilled shadows. Blankets had been set out, along with fruits, cheese, bread, nuts, and drink.

"Jordan, what is all this for?"

"This is the birthday present I really wanted, time alone with you, here in this place. Just in case you were tired, hungry, or thirsty, I wanted to be prepared for everything. I want to spend the night here with you like we did when you visited me."

"Jordan, you know what almost happened here the last time. Are you sure this is a good idea?"

"Annaliessa, if you can stay here with me tonight, in my arms, I will have the hope that we can indeed be married. I will know that you are ready to accept all the love I have to share with you, in all the forms that expression takes. Does that make you worried or nervous in any way?"

"Astonishingly, no," I stated. "I am not nervous or worried. I would like to engage in your experiment, as I am eager to know where I stand on this matter."

"Good, then join me on the blankets."

He did not push to make our time more intimate immediately. He let me warm to the place, and our conversation. We lay in each others arms and it felt like when we were in the beech tree after my birthday. I had no fear, only the overwhelming urge to have him near me like this always.

I shifted to my side and propped my head up on my bent arm so I could look at his handsome face. I placed my other hand on his cheek and felt tingles shoot down my arm. I heard him gasp a little, as he was surprised by my initiative. Before I could change my mind I leaned down and kissed him. It was not the sweet and gentle kind that we had shared recently, but a hungry, demanding kind, and he responded zealously. He gave me admittance and claimed my tongue as if it was a wild beast to be tamed.

I felt him shift to his side and he pulled me to him. His hands were raking down my back until he finally latched onto my buttocks and ground his loins against my body. He was rigid already, and the moans that escaped his lips set me on fire. I felt myself throbbing between my legs in an ardent way. I could not get close enough to him, and I was starting to feel greedy with want.

I pushed him onto his back and straddled him. My soft folds of womanhood were pressed against his engorged penis. I felt myself pushing against him, and the pleasure it was creating was delightful. I felt my gown dampen from the moisture that was already building, as my body was preparing to welcome him in and entertain every fantasy of sensuousness it could afford.

Our kisses were scorching heat-filled depths of wonder, and I could feel his hand on my breast, as he played with my alert nipple. His other hand was on my hip and he was using that as leverage to press himself against me in a more rhythmic pattern.

I wanted to explore every inch of this man and have him delve into the discovery of how to make me reach the pinnacle of rapturous bliss.

Yes, I think I have come full circle. I think I am ready to be his wife, and to be joined in every way possible. I want to know him like no one else can, and I want him to know every fiber of my being.

I broke our kiss, and sat upright, and reached my hand up to the clasp on my gown to undo it. Jordan saw my intent, and reached up his hand to stop me.

"Annaliessa, no! As much as I want this right now, and I really want this with you, I will not rob us our first night as a married couple. I had not intended to have things get this out of hand, but the thrill of having you respond to me this way, is more than I could bear."

"Are you sure you want to risk saying no to me again, Jordan?" I teased.

"No, I am not sure at all, and every part of me wants to say yes. It wants to say yes urgently, and in all kinds of ways. You cannot imagine how torn I am at this moment. My mind is telling me to stop, but my body is telling me to let you keep going. Annaliessa, I want you to have everything you deserve, and by cheating you of that now, I feel I will be disappointing you."

"Jordan, you are anything but a disappointment to me. You are the most amazing man, and I want to be your wife, forever and always. If that means I have to wait a few more cycles of the moon, then I will wait. At least I know without a doubt that I can have the intimacy with you that couples should share, and that is a victory."

"You want to be my wife? Did I really just hear you say that? You mean it, right?"

"Of course I mean it! Do you know me to be in the habit of saying things I do not mean?"

"Annaliessa, I need you to stand up."

"What? You want me to stand up? Why?"

"Please, just do it."

I reluctantly pushed myself off of him. I could not deny his request. He had patiently waited for me, so this was the least I could do.

I stood, and he rolled over and grabbed something from his coat pocket, and then rolled back over and up onto one knee.

"Annaliessa, would you do me the honor of being my wife?" He opened the box that contained a beautiful sapphire and emerald ring. The sapphire was cut into a heart shape and the emeralds formed a ring around the outer edge of it. I had never seen anything so beautiful.

"Jordan, it would be my honor to be your wife."

He stood with his face glowing, placed the ring on my finger and then lifted me into his arms and swung me around in an exuberant display of giddiness. When he planted my feet back down on the ground, he bent down and kissed me in such a way as to stamp ownership on my lips.

"How soon can I make you my wife?"

"If it were up to me, I would say tonight, but of course, there are all the rigors of proper society that we must adhere to. There is also Samuel's upcoming wedding that we cannot overshadow, so that means the time of the tree budding at the earliest."

"I cannot wait until then. I will never be able to withstand the temptation that long," he said pleadingly.

"The only option is to elope. Our families and kingdoms will be devastated, but we will be happy."

"In a fortnight then. I cannot bear to wait any longer than that.

"Actually, that will work. Josiah turns seventeen years a fortnight hence. We can secretly marry in Dilentis when we travel to his kingdom for his birthday."

"I will arrange to have a cleric officiate our vows the night before his party. Perhaps we can enlist Josiah's help, and he can be a witness to our covenant. I am sure Evirent, Seraphina, or Cassia would be willing to aid us in our endeavor as well. I will contact them, and will speak to Josiah upon our arrival in Dilentis."

"Agreed. I too cannot wait to be by your side as your wife. I do not want to risk anything happening that would put a stop to it. Jordan, as hard as this is for me to give up, I do not think I should wear the ring until the day you put it on my finger as your wife. Otherwise, people will be watchful, and plans will be set in motion that neither one of us will be able cancel."

"Very wise insight. I will keep it close to my heart until then. Would you join me in a drink to celebrate our engagement?"

The rest of the night drifted past in an ecstatic state of awareness. We reveled in the warmth of each other's arms. Contentment had settled our spirits and we were going to be knit together as one, a bonded cord that could not be severed by adversity, strife, or evil.

Return Visit

43

It had been seven days since we had made our plan, and though it was difficult, we tried not to be alone together, so we would not succumb to our fleshly lusts. The draw to entertain the enchantment of its trapping was arduous, but the sweet triumph of our faithfulness was within reach, and we both wanted the crown of victory; our wedding night to be everything it was meant to be. In fact, it would mean so much more given the jagged terrain of trials and emotions that had to be traversed to get there.

That morning, I was walking through the freshly fallen snow of the grounds while I waited for Jordan to be finished with his duties to the kingdom. I rounded a hedge, and collided with Brian. He caught me before I fell into the snow, and I felt a shiver run through me.

"Princess Annaliessa, I apologize for not paying more heed to where I was going. I heard you had been staying here since the sun's zenith, but I was not sure when I would actually have the pleasure of your company. It is quite fortunate I was able to have this unplanned coincidence."

"Brian, I was not aware you were planning on a visit," I said rather stiffly, but not meaning to be rude.

"I thought I would visit for a few days here before heading to Dilentis for Prince Josiah's celebration."

"Well, it is nice that you are able to come and spend some time with your extended family."

"Princess Annaliessa, I feel there are things left unsaid between us, and I cannot bear to leave them as such."

"Brian, there is nothing that needs to be said."

"I beg to differ. I want to make sure you understand that I had no idea you would choose the path you did when I had that talk with you. If I had known you would go to those lengths to avoid your father's manipulation of power, I would have remained silent; that I assure you. It was never my intention to cause you or my cousin such acute pain. It sickened me when I discovered what you were planning to do. I will never forgive myself for what happened."

"Brian, I hold no grudge against you. I have worked through forgiveness, and I understand that I could have chosen a different path and procured the support of others. That decision is all my own, so you bear no guilt in it. Please accept my forgiveness if it will help you release yourself from that blame, and I am sorry to have made you feel the burden of that responsibility. It was not yours to carry."

"You are exquisite, Your Highness. A true treasure, one so rare, a man would be willing to give up everything he owns in order to secure it for himself."

"Thank you, but your accolades are far too generous for me."

"Has my cousin been successful in courting your emotions? If he cannot persuade you soon, I fear he will have to fight off a large battalion of men who would like that distinction."

"You flatter me, Brian. I am sure you have exaggerated your compliment to a great degree."

"You have no idea, do you?"

"What are you talking about?"

"There are still hundreds of men who want the opportunity to win your hand and have been grumbling quite profusely as of late how Prince Jordan is monopolizing all of your time. Some did remove their names from the list after the incident with Tyson, but many were even more adamant about having the opportunity to win your affections."

"I have heard none of this. How can this be?"

"My cousin is resourceful when it comes to getting what he wants. It is no secret that the only thing he wants is you as his wife."

"Yes, he has made that clear to me as well."

"So you are still resisting his manly charm and charisma?"

"I hate to disappoint my subjects, but I will not be contemplating a marriage with anyone but Jordan. We will be wed. It is only a matter of time."

"So he has officially proposed?"

"He proposes to me practically every day. If it were up to him, we would have been married already."

"So why do you deny him his desire?"

"Have you not heard the saying, 'There is a time and a season for everything'?"

"Yes, of course, but which season is the one that has your attention?"

"That is a question I will have to leave unanswered. You will know when everyone else does, and not a moment before."

"You are teasing me now, Your Highness. You know exactly when it will be. I can see it on your face."

"Jordan should be finishing with his business, and I really must excuse myself. It was rewarding to have cleared up any misunderstanding that might exist between us. I wish you much success and happiness in your future activities."

I know he was not happy with me brushing aside his question, but I was not going to risk it. Jordan and I were to be married in mere days, and that was the only thing I was focused on. I could not afford any distractions, and he had a proven history of throwing things into confusion, mostly me.

Ally Procurement

44

I was on pins and needles during the trek to Dilentis. Jordan had assured me that the cleric was being readied at this hour. He did not know who he was marrying, but he was told it was a union that needed to be official quickly. This was not unheard of when young girls found themselves with child, and I am sure this would be his assumption. I could not wait to see the look on his face when Jordan and I walk into the chapel.

Cassia was going to help us leave the castle if a diversion was necessary. She was not sure how to accomplish the task, but was certain she could improvise if needed.

All that was left was for Jordan to speak with Josiah as soon as we arrived at the castle. He would make it easy for us to leave without being questioned, and his support would be an asset.

After what felt like a lifetime, we finally arrived. We were greeted by one of King Darius' trusted advisors and shown to our rooms. Jordan asked for word to be sent to Josiah that he wished to see him right away.

It did not take long for Josiah to respond. He was being bored with the details of the party protocols for tomorrow, and was delighted to have a diversion. He went straight to Jordan's room without hesitation, and was surprised to see me there as well.

"Jordan and Annaliessa, it is good to see you again. I was disappointed you did not have to endure the torture that is a royal birthday. Tell me your secret in avoiding them; I will employ it next year."

Laughing, Jordan said, "No secret. I have the best reason in the world. Annaliessa. She hates public festivities right now, and my parents are quite accommodating when my requests revolve around her."

"So what you are telling me is that I need to find myself enraptured by a beautiful woman?"

"You need to find yourself a wife."

"You seem to be lacking one still. Why should I rush into something with a stranger that you have been unsuccessful in procuring with the love of your life?"

"No offense, Annaliessa, but with all the time you two spend together, it amazes me you two have not made any kind of announcement," he stated as an afterthought, remembering I was in the room.

"That is what I wanted to talk to you about. I plan on marrying Annaliessa tonight. We are eloping and I need your help to get out of the castle. We would like you to stand with us as our witness."

Josiah looked over to me for confirmation, and I nodded my head.

"You are joking, right? You know the scandal an elopement will cause. Surely, not even what happened to Annaliessa would keep you from the consequences of that deed, unless you have to marry her for family reasons," he said a bit uncomfortably.

"I have not exercised any marital type of benefits with her if that is what you are implying. I will deal with the consequences. I only want one thing, and that is to be wed to her, and waiting for the proper channels to align is far too distant of a timeframe. I have already waited far longer than I ever intended. Will you support us?"

"I want to ensure that you know it is your bloodbath, and not mine. You will take all of the blame, and that means you coerced me into helping you if pressed for explanations. Are we clear?"

"Like I said, I will deal with the consequences. In the end, it is what everyone expects and wishes to happen. They will only be upset about not being there to witness it. We can throw a big party later when the trees start to bloom, to officially commemorate the union. We have another way to commemorate it tonight that has far more meaning to us than a party."

I was seriously blushing after that last statement, and hoped Josiah would not glance over in my direction.

"I hope one day I will know the desire that drives you to this insanity. I am sure it will be worth it since you love each other so dearly."

We spent the next half hour discussing when and how he would get us out of the castle.

Elopement

45

Josiah told everyone he was taking us on a walk around the grounds. There was a spot by the river that he was fond of fishing at and wanted Jordan to know its location so he could spend time in the rewarding recreation of fishing while he was at Dilentis.

It was dark and there was much dissention about us going at this hour, but Jordan assured everyone that Cassia was going to be with us, and she would be security enough. Josiah stated that there was something about being in the woods and staring up at the stars at night that he just could not get during the day, and besides, tomorrow he would be busy preparing for the party.

Our parents reluctantly agreed, but they knew Josiah was well acquainted with the wooded path that lead to the river and felt reassured that we had a dragon along for company.

When we got to the river, three horses were there for us to make our journey into town. We wasted no time taking a leisurely ride. We galloped as fast as the horses would take us.

We were at the chapel in about a half hour. Prince Josiah went and knocked at the parsonage door. The cleric answered, and when he saw the prince, he was taken aback. Josiah said the couple was with him and waiting at the front door to the chapel. He was providing aid as it was a dear friend of his needing to marry quickly.

The cleric said he would open the front door in a couple of minutes and that Prince Josiah should come inside and take the private entry to the chapel so as not to arouse any suspicion should someone pass by.

We held hands and could scarcely believe we were actually going to be married tonight. Everything we had ever hoped for was bound up in our life together, and we just wanted to start living it.

Josiah opened the front door and we walked in. The cleric was at the altar and had his back to the door. We approached the front of the chapel quietly and quickly.

The cleric was placing his religious attire on when he turned to greet the couple. His mouth hung open in surprise. He stuttered, trying to get words to form, but could not make his lips and tongue work properly. "Y-y-you are t-t-t-the couple who is in trouble?"

"Trouble can be defined quite broadly. We need to get married, and you have been selected to perform the ceremony that will make us so," stated Jordan matter-of-factly.

"Where are your parents? Should they not be here?"

"We are both of legal age to marry. They want us to be married, and have no misgivings about our union, or we would not be here." *This was partially true, but not entirely. I was not going to point out that the statement contained only the implied truth and not the absolute truth.*

Perhaps a female voice would break his shock and produce the much needed action. "Can we begin the ceremony, please?"

"Very well then, Josiah, are you acting as witness to this covenant?"

"Yes, I will testify to their union and to their love for each other."

Without all the normal royal procedures, the ceremony was very brief. I shed tears when Jordan declared his vows and placed the ring back on my finger. He had tears in his eyes as well. The cleric pronounced us husband and wife, and Jordan took me in his arms and kissed me perfunctorily.

He whispered in my ear, "I do not want to give the cleric anything to gossip about if asked to describe our kiss." This of course, made me smile and giggle a little.

The chapel registry was completed, providing a written copy of our union. It was rewarding to see our signatures along with Josiah's and the cleric's on the page. Jordan had scribed an official kingdom document, and we all put our signatures onto that parchment as well. It was official. We were married, and nothing could change it. Small chapels like this one could not afford the parchment to provide individual marriage documents, thus the registry was initiated and kept at the chapel for inspection.

We paid the cleric handsomely for his time, and asked him to keep the union silent until it could be announced at tomorrow's party. Josiah did not mind that it would upstage his party. He was willing to have anything else take the spotlight, and he said the fallout from the announcement was going to be well worth it.

We rode hard back to the woods and a stable hand was there to collect the horses. We walked back to the castle with a spring in our step, as we knew what was ahead of us that night.

Discovery

46

When we arrived at the castle, our parents were waiting for us to join them in discussions. We did our duty, but were very distracted. I had pulled the ring off my finger and had it hidden in a pocket inside my coat which had been taken to my room.

We were all finally excused, and Jordan and I headed to my room. Josiah was not going to tell anyone we were together; he did not want to ruin the surprise. Josiah actually joined us in my room for a few minutes to make it look like we were all conversing so as not to draw any suspicion on Jordan. He waited for the corridor to be clear and then took his leave. If anyone questioned him, he would state that Jordan was already in his room.

I had my ring out of my pocket and back on my finger. I could not help but admire it. It was the symbol of our union, and it meant a great deal to me.

I heard Evirent calling to me. Apparently, Jordan did, too, by the look he was giving me.

"I am speaking to both of you, so you will both know the information I am sharing with you. It is very important, and only the two of you can know it. Do you understand?"

Both Jordan and I nodded our heads at the same time we sent out a *"Yes, we understand,"* to Evirent.

"Now that you are married and the likelihood that you will produce children is high, there is something you need to know about how the dragon blood will pass to your children."

Jordan and I had never given much thought to how what we shared individually would impact our children. We were a bit nervous, given all the hurdles we had jumped to get to this point.

"Your children will be unique. They will have the blood of two dragons coursing through their bodies as well as your own. They will be stronger, faster, smarter, and overall better than an average human. In fact, they will be able to wield magic, but must be taught that this is only to be used in cases of emergency and for good. If they allow it to corrupt them, they will die untimely deaths. When the time comes to instruct them in their magic abilities, I will teach them. They will not come into their magic power until they reach thirteen years. Until then, you should not speak of this ability. In fact, how they are different should not be spoken of at all. Evil men will try to take advantage of their exceptional attributes for their gain if it is common knowledge. Do you understand the seriousness of what I am sharing with you, and will you do as I have instructed?"

"Yes, we understand and will do exactly what you have asked of us." Jordan and I both had our eyebrows raised in amazement. Only we could have something with so great a responsibility placed on our shoulders. Becoming a mother seemed daunting enough, but this was overwhelming.

Evirent bid us farewell. Both Jordan and I sat down on the bed with a stiff, statue-like pose.

"Annaliessa, I know this seems like it is something out of a fairy tale. We have been entrusted with a great gift, and with power responsibility comes as well. Something we are both aware of intimately. I do not think we should worry ourselves with something that will work itself out as we continue on in our lives. We have each other, and together we will be able to handle this and what comes from it."

"You still have not lost your touch in knowing what to say to make me feel better," I said with a thankful smile. "I believe we have some unfinished business to take care of tonight, and that is the only thing I want to focus on right now."

Announcement

47

That night was the most romantic, exhilarating, and liberating of my life. We had joined ourselves in the most profound way two people can. Jordan made it everything I had hoped it would be, and I for him. I was not going to tire anytime soon in exploring the exotic contours of his muscled body and the way we fit together so perfectly. The titillating sensation of those cascading waves of orgasmic climax was etched into my memory, and I craved the release that it brought. I could hardly think of anything else but how I would never be the same if I could not have it again. I was hooked, and weaning myself off was not an option. Thankfully, Jordan did not deny me, and he took me to that place of euphoria multiple times last night. My body ached from the physical exertion of our love making, but it was a good ache, satisfying.

Since we never slept that night, we rose early so that Jordan could go to his room and prepare for the day ahead. It was a day that had us both a little anxious.

We managed to stay clear of our parents until dinner. This was where the news would be delivered, and we hoped it would be met with joy.

Josiah had spread the news to the other princes, and they all had congratulated us. They did not envy what lay before us at dinner, but said that we had their support.

Everyone was seated when Jordan and I walked into the dining hall hand-in-hand. This garnered stunned looks from the older generation. Of course, they did not know we were married, so it was not as scandalous as it appeared.

Jordan and I approached the table and found we were not seated next to each other. My mother took one look at me and gasped audibly. "Annaliessa, what have you done?" It was a question, but it came out more like an exclamation.

She stood and walked up to me, taking my left hand in hers and glared at the ring that spoke of our union, and not just our betrothal. "You two have become engaged without the consent of either of your families and the formalities that are custom?"

"No, mother, not engaged, married."

The sound of people choking on their drinks and stunned intakes of breath immediately permeated the room, and then silence as the reality of my statement took hold.

"You were married? When? By whom?"

"Last night. In town, at the chapel, by the cleric. We have the official documentation to prove that we are legally and morally wed."

My mother, not wanting everyone to hear her next question leaned in and whispered in my ear, "Have you consummated this union?" I only had to smile for her to understand the answer was affirmative.

"Annaliessa, how could you be so neglectful in fulfilling your obligations to societal protocols and expectations? It is not that we are not happy to see you wed, it is that you did it in secret."

King Darius spoke up. "Josiah, were you part of this plan? Did you aid them in this elopement?"

"King Darius, if I may interject," stated Jordan, "I forced Josiah to assist us. I should bear any consequences for our actions. He is without blame."

"I fail to see how you could have forced him to do something so disdainful."

"He owed me a favor, and last night I collected on it. He could not refuse."

King Darius turned to his son, "Is this true Josiah?"

"Yes, father, it is."

King Nicolas stood, and came forward to stand before his son. "Jordan, this is not how you were raised to do things. In fact, you have never given us cause for concern before. You have always been most upright with scrupulous morals. If the first time you have erred is to marry the woman you have loved and waited for patiently, then I find that I can extend you pardon. You answered to the higher standard of what is right, as I am assuming you two did not marry to cover up an indiscretion, but you married for love, correct?"

"Yes, father, we married for love. We remained steadfast until we had exchanged our vows. I wanted to do things properly. I just did not want to risk losing her again, and was not willing to let fate have an opportunity to destroy our happiness that following protocol might have provided. Surely, based on history, you can understand this reasoning?"

King Nicolas bent so that he could speak privately to the two of us, "I know the temptation a looming wedding night brings. I certainly am not going to cast the first stone."

He then took me into an enthusiastic embrace and then put Jordan into one as well.

Queen Sarah followed my mother in giving us her blessing, and then the others followed and lifted their voices in assent. Everyone was overjoyed that we were married, just not impressed with how we did it.

That night, at the party, the news spread like a wild fire and we were engulfed with well-wishers.

We were tired and felt the drain of no sleep quickly catching up to us. We excused ourselves and returned to my room, no longer worried about being discovered.

We made love and fell asleep wrapped in each other's arms. The feel of his nakedness against me would have aroused that craving to be satisfied yet again if I were not so exhausted. We were married, and we would have many nights to delve into the wonders of each other's bodies, and with that, I drifted into a sound sleep.

The End